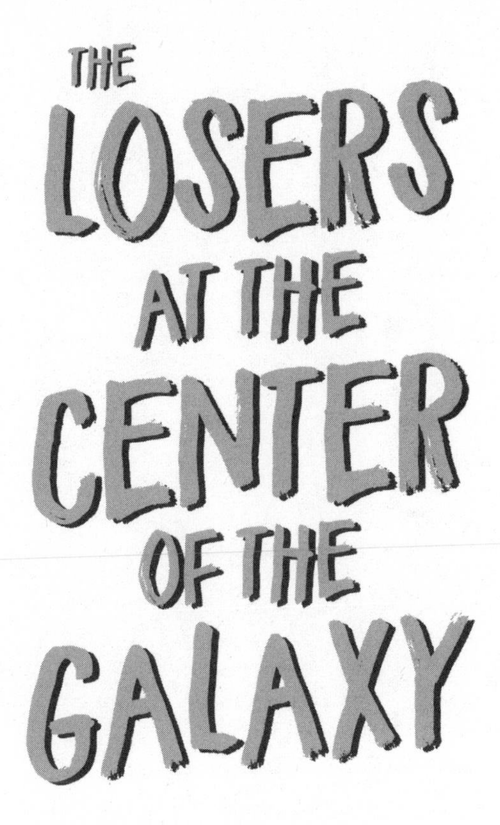
THE
LOSERS
AT THE
CENTER
OF THE
GALAXY

The Losers at the Center of the Galaxy

MARY WINN HEIDER

LITTLE, BROWN AND COMPANY
NEW YORK BOSTON

Little, Brown and Company
Hachette Book Group
1290 Avenue of the Americas, New York, NY 10104
Visit us at LBYR.com

First Edition: March 2021

Little, Brown and Company is a division of Hachette Book Group, Inc. The Little, Brown name and logo are trademarks of Hachette Book Group, Inc.

The publisher is not responsible for websites (or their content) that are not owned by the publisher.

Library of Congress Cataloging-in-Publication Data
Names: Heider, Mary Winn, author.
Title: The losers at the center of the galaxy / Mary Winn Heider.
Description: First edition. | New York; Boston: Little, Brown and Company, 2021. | Audience: Ages 8-12. | Summary: Two years after their father disappeared, Winston and Louise wrestle with their grief while investigating mysterious teachers, innovative science, and a captive bear.
Identifiers: LCCN 2020040280 | ISBN 9780759555426 (hardcover) | ISBN 9780759555419 (ebook)
Subjects: CYAC: Brothers and sisters—Fiction. | Middle schools—Fiction. | Schools—Fiction. | Missing persons—Fiction. | Humorous stories.
Classification: LCC PZ7.1.H443 Los 2021b | DDC [Fic]—dc23
LC record available at https://lccn.loc.gov/2020040280

ISBNs: 978-0-7595-5542-6 (hardcover),
978-0-7595-5541-9 (ebook)

Printed in the United States of America

LSC-C

Printing 1, 2021

FOR JOHN AND PAUL,
THE ORIGINAL BUZZARDS

CHAPTER 1

WINSTON AND LOUISE stood together at the fifty-yard line.

The center of the entire galaxy.

It was a weird place to put the center of the galaxy, to be honest. The ground was squishy, the air smelled like armpit, and the crowd roared.

Also, the cheerleaders were on fire.

Winston saw the flames shooting up from the squad, and his only thought was that he needed to protect his little sister, so without giving it another thought, he up and tackled Louise. It was the first thing that had occurred to him, and if he'd waited just long enough for a *second* thing to occur to him, he probably would have realized it was a bad idea. Pretty much immediately, he knew it was not going over well.

"Win*ston*!" Louise yelled as she hit the ground. A herd of halftime crew stampeded past, and she pushed her brother over onto the spongy turf and stood, shoving her bangs out of her eyes. "*Come on,* Win."

Winston glanced back toward the cheerleaders, prepared to try to protect Louise again, but he noticed that they were still cheering. That was unexpected, coming from a bunch of people who were supposedly on fire, but then they spun around and he saw that they were *not* on fire. Not at all. They were wearing upside-down jet packs or something. It was a stunt.

He stood quickly, taking his place next to Louise. "I thought they were on fire," he said, trying to explain. "I didn't want you to see—"

"You have to stop doing that," Louise said, brushing off her funeral clothes.

Just a few hours ago, she'd yelled at their mom from behind her bedroom door, hollered, *It's not a funeral*, before eventually giving up and slouching out in black pants and a gray sweater. Winston decided now was not the time to point out that at least funeral clothes didn't show grass stains.

"I'm only trying to help," he mumbled.

"I know," Louise said, rolling her eyes. "But you are *not* helping. You're ruining all my pants."

"But—"

"*Stop. Helping.*"

Winston nodded reluctantly. They both needed tonight to go well.

Here at the center of the galaxy.

Their dad had called it that.

And not just because of the hot dogs, he used to say, winking.

If it had been up to Winston, the center of the galaxy would be more like Stonehenge but bigger, a whole planet full of mysterious and ancient cold rocks that nobody understood. Or else somewhere that burned nonstop, like a sun.

Not here, on Earth, where the stadium lights blazed in his eyes, people kept bumping into him, and the Chicago Horribles were losing by fifty-nine points already even though it was only halftime.

But his dad had called this the center of the galaxy, and so here they were.

The booming chaos of the stadium swirled around them, and Winston hoped no one noticed his freak out. People were everywhere, shouting into walkie-talkies and moving things and waving to *other* people across the field.

A few feet over, Winston and Louise's mom was deep in conversation with the police detective, while a man with a headset adjusted a podium in front of them. Since they'd first arrived, escorted through the tunnels and then out under the enormous CHICAGO URSUS ARCTOS HORRIBLES archway, no one paid much attention to them, the two kids of the missing quarterback. *Former* quarterback. It was obvious that nobody knew what to say to them, that they made people uncomfortable. So they kept to themselves and watched it all happening around them: golf carts zooming, the now-extinguished cheerleaders pouncing and tossing each other in the air, and at one end zone, the stage going up for a band that would play when they were done.

A mic check boomed from somewhere, and the siblings inched closer to each other. Winston was a year older and only barely taller—from the stands they probably looked like the same person, copied and pasted side by side. They both had dark curly hair that they kept short and square chins that they kept set. They had pale skin and freckles that kept them out of the sun. They had their dad's broad, made-for-football shoulders.

Winston and Louise looked like they were built to stop things.

Except, of course, they hadn't been able to stop anything. That was what had brought them to the stadium tonight. The complete and total inability to stop their dad from disappearing.

It had been three weeks.

Twenty-one days since he'd just walked away.

And in a minute, they were going to ask for help from everybody watching—the fans in the stadium and the fans on their sofas at home. The incomplete Volpe family would send up a flare, and their dad would find his way back home, either on his own, or because some nice stranger would see him and recognize him and know he should be returned to his family, even if he didn't remember that himself. It was going to work. It had to work.

So. There Winston stood, at the galactic bull's-eye of hopefulness. That alone was bound to make a person jumpy, especially around flaming cheerleaders.

He closed his eyes, shutting out the stadium full of people.

When his dad had been quarterback of the Chicago Horribles, he'd stood right here. Right here on this exact same squishy ground. He had felt the pressure of a whole stadium of people looking down on him. He'd told Winston once that when the pressure was too distracting and he needed to be calm inside, he would close his eyes out there and imagine someone gently pouring water on his head. At the time, Winston hadn't understood how that would work exactly, but he tried it now, and he had the very distinct sensation that *he'd* been on fire and just didn't realize it until right this second. Gradually, he felt his insides calm down.

His dad had been right about the water trick.

"Did it help you win games?" Winston had asked him.

And his dad had laughed, a great round laugh. He'd pulled Winston into a hug, the safe, forever kind. "Oh, sweetheart." His dad chuckled. "I never won. But I had a lot more fun losing."

Winston wished he could remember seeing his dad play.

A loud groan made him open his eyes. He and

Louise turned around at the same time. There was a bear on the ground behind them.

Then Winston's brain kicked in, and it wasn't a bear, of course, it was a football player—one of the current Chicago Horribles. They'd gotten new uniforms, with fake bear heads that pulled up and over the helmets.

"Get a cart," the guy moaned, clutching his shin.

Winston glanced around, realizing that the golf carts weren't just zipping around the field for fun, they were collecting players too banged up to limp into the tunnels by themselves.

He waved his arms, and it took a few minutes, but eventually one of the carts headed his way. As he turned back, Winston saw that Louise was kneeling beside the guy, with a hand on his forehead.

She was saying something to him.

Winston wanted to join them, but whatever was happening seemed private, so he stayed where he was, awkwardly pointing as if the people driving the cart didn't know where they were going. When they pulled up, Louise got back to her feet, a strange look on her face. She didn't tell Winston what she'd talked about with the man, and he didn't ask.

Just then, a hush fell over the crowd and the

JumboTrons lit up with the Volpes' faces. It was a shock to see the giant, looming version of himself a hundred feet in the air.

"You two ready?" their mom asked.

A wave of nerves crashed over Winston, but he nodded. It was time. He noticed that Louise was still fixed on the cart with that injured player, watching as it disappeared into the shadows of the tunnel.

He nudged her, and she nudged him back, just as a few more people stepped up on the other side of the detective. Behind their little group, a semicircle formed—all the former players they could bring together at such short notice, guys who'd played when Lenny Volpe was quarterback.

Winston tried to see traces of his father in the men, but then, too quickly, he had to turn around and face the cameras.

It was on.

The press conference started with the detective. It was a good choice, whoever decided that, and the crowd fell silent as she painted the picture of a hero lost in time and space, done in by his own broken mind. Her voice boomed into the stands as she asked for information related to the disappearance of Lenny Volpe.

Next up was their mom, telling the story of the day he left. That he kissed them all goodbye and walked out. It was a made-up story, but only Winston and Louise knew that, and it was the sort of story people wanted to hear. Plus, it had already been on TV, in the paper. What made today different was the next speaker. He was the key. He was the one the public would listen to. He was the one Winston's dad might listen to, if that was possible anymore. He had the specific kind of power that comes with owning an entire football team, even if it is the worst football team in the whole country.

He stepped up to the podium.

The owner of the Chicago Horribles leaned into the microphone.

And then he opened his mouth and made a joke. A joke about how Lenny Volpe must've dropped a few marbles to have forgotten how great he had it, and he waved toward Winston and Louise and their mom, but Winston didn't want to be part of that joke, and all the hope he'd had poured out of him as Louise leapt, like a coiled-up long jumper, straight toward the man, and more specifically, toward his nose, which she headbutted with impressive force.

The man's nose started bleeding immediately.

The crowd roared their approval.

Winston was so surprised his mouth dropped open, and he watched as the man swore and tried to stop his bloody nose with somebody else's tie. Around him, the old players muttered under their breath about Louise and that leap, that real stunner of a jump considering how she was a kid.

"Holy smokes..."

"Lenny Volpe's kid, all right..."

"Five bucks says she could sky you..."

"Not taking any chances, thanks..."

The man's nose spurted even more vigorously, and he yelled about it being broken. The crowd cheered impossibly louder, and Winston felt the sound surge against him like a wave. He might be crushed by all those eyes on him, all that noise. His chest felt tight. It was hard to breathe. This was wrong. This wasn't the way it was supposed to happen. He was aware of everything all at once, how every person on the field closed in on them by a few feet, of his own embarrassing face, high up and giant on the JumboTron. Next to him, their mom was leaning over Louise, half scolding her, half making sure she was okay.

Louise caught Winston's eye and gave him a crooked smile.

She'd been right. She didn't need him to save her. She could do just fine on her own, and he didn't understand why, but it made him even sadder.

The press conference ended pretty quickly after that.

Incredibly, the Chicago Horribles dominated in the second half. They won by a single point.

A couple of weeks later, Winston was assigned the tuba in band and learned to play Darth Vader's theme song.

Louise turned her attention to science.

And Lenny Volpe stayed missing.

CHAPTER 2

Two Years Later

WINSTON SAT IN the cafeteria of Subito School, ignoring his bologna sandwich and humming Darth Vader's theme song.

Yesterday, he'd gotten inspired and composed some words to go along with the melody of "The Imperial March," so now he was running through it in his head:

HEY, IT'S ME
I'M YOUR DAD
I'M YOUR DAD

Pure poetry.

HEY, IT'S ME
I'M YOUR DAD
I'M YOUR DAD

To be very clear, though, his love for the song had nothing to do with his *own* dad or the disappearance or the memory of ever watching *Star Wars* with his dad or literally anything at all like that. It was because Winston was a tuba player. And "The Imperial March" was like breathing to a tuba player.

That was all it was.

HEY, IT'S ME
I'M YOUR DAD
I'M YOUR DAD

He was still humming to himself when, across the cafeteria, Frenchie LeGume stepped through the door to the hot lunch line and out of sight, and for a second, Winston had the distinct feeling that a black hole had just swallowed a star. *Bloop.* He blinked after her and then shook it off, feeling his cheeks go hot. It wasn't like him to be so dramatic about . . . well . . . the hot lunch line.

Okay, fine.

It was.

It was like Winston to be dramatic about everything. Everything except Louise, because she didn't like it and told him so.

But it wasn't like he *tried.* Without meaning to, he could imagine the worst thing. Even the most ridiculous worst thing, like the time a bee flew past him on the walk to school, and he thought, *What if I swallowed that bee?* and then he spent the rest of the day not talking because of the imaginary bee-swallowing incident.

He'd been dramatic about the house. When they had to put the house up for sale, he'd spent entire weekends going from room to room, closing his eyes, and quizzing himself on what it looked like, just to make sure he wouldn't forget. And when the doorbell rang one afternoon, and he answered to find a nice-looking man rubbing his hands together in the cold, a man who politely inquired after the *For Sale by Owner* sign taped to the window, Winston yelled, "IT'S MY HOUSE, YOU CAN'T HAVE IT!" and slammed the door in his face.

He felt bad about it later, when the house didn't sell, and *still* didn't sell, and he watched his mom get a wrinkle in the middle of her forehead that never went away anymore. It was probably hard enough being a real estate agent who couldn't even sell your own house—it was definitely harder when your own kid was sabotaging you.

Winston liked using dramatic words like *sabotage*.

But he was probably most dramatic about the tuba. From the very first day, he'd felt like the tuba was a long-lost piece of himself that he'd finally found. In fact, he was so dramatic about the tuba that one time in band class while Mr. Manning had been working with the saxophones, Winston's mind drifted and he thought to himself, *This tuba has kept me alive for the last two years*, and then almost burst into tears with the truth of it, and if the saxophones had not, at that moment, played a really horrible note all in unison, he might well have. Because really, if it weren't for the tuba, he might have died of loneliness. Louise had disappeared into after-school activities. His mom had disappeared into being a real estate agent. His dad, of course, had just straight-up disappeared.

So he'd filled the empty house with the sound of the tuba. He'd lug the school loaner home most days of the week, sit in the kitchen, and practice. One of those days, he'd gotten up for some water and then turned at the sink to see his tuba right where he'd left it, sitting in the chair, waiting for him. The light from the window fell across the brass, and it shone there in the middle of the kitchen, alone, and golden, and perfect, and Winston felt his heart expand to the precise size of a tuba.

Somehow, the tuba understood what it meant to be alone.

So he named the tuba the Lonesome (it felt exactly dramatic enough), and that very afternoon he'd accidentally played the first few notes of "The Imperial March." Then he'd picked out the next few notes, playing and playing and playing, filling the house with the velvety sounds of Vader's empire until Louise had appeared in the doorway, hours before she was usually home.

She wandered in, leaning against the wall by the oven, absently picking at a singed bit of paint from long ago, and listened to him play.

"You sound like whale farts," she said when he stopped.

"At least I don't *smell* like whale farts," he said brightly. Then, quickly, so she didn't misunderstand, he said, "I mean, not that *you* do. As far as we know. Who even knows what whale farts smell like?"

"Fish, I guess."

He considered that. "Fish know? Or the farts smell like fish?"

"Where's Mom?" she asked, and for the billionth time, he wondered why she always felt like the older one.

He pointed toward the middle of the fridge, where the note their mom left had partially slid down. All their magnets were dying. "Scheduling showings for some other agent. Why're you home so early?"

She opened the fridge door and grabbed some bologna. "Dr. O had a dentist appointment. She sent me home."

"You're the only one in Science Club now?"

"No," she said, exasperated. "But the rest of them didn't care enough to try to get her to move the appointment. They aren't actual scientists. They just like setting hair spray on fire."

"That sounds . . . kind of fun."

"Science Club isn't supposed to be *fun*," she said, and without another word, she left, slamming into her room, and he hugged the Lonesome closer, wondering what he'd said wrong. He probably shouldn't have said anything. Or maybe just stuck to whale farts.

If a whale farted in the ocean and nobody was around to hear it, did it make a noise?

Well, the whale heard it, at least.

He started playing again, quietly, so it wouldn't bother Louise in her room. Sometimes, playing quietly was just as dramatic as playing loudly. When no one was home, though, which was nearly every day after school until the evening, he played his whole heart out. On the worst days, when the house seemed emptiest, the sound was inarguable proof he was, at the very least, still alive.

If he'd been a whale, this was him, hearing his own farts.

That was what the tuba had given him.

That and Frenchie.

And Frenchie was . . . also a big part of currently being alive.

Now, in the cafeteria, he watched as she threaded her way over to where he sat. Her high ponytail switched as she dodged someone with a teetering tray of milks. Someone, probably a new kid, stared a little too long as she passed. When Winston had first met her, he thought she'd had birthmarks scattered across her face and arms—later she told him, just once, with the matter-of-factness she might have told him her class schedule, that it was a whole thing, that her skin lost pigment in the sun, here and there, without any pattern or reason. Permanently.

It was one of two things they didn't talk about. The disappearance was the other.

She slid into the seat next to him, her tray fitting neatly beside his, so that the two of them looked out at the cafeteria in front of them. It was the way they always sat, Frenchie on the left, Winston on the right, a habit they picked up from band, where she was first chair tuba and he was second chair tuba.

Frenchie was the only person who knew he'd named his tuba the Lonesome. He'd told her at this exact table.

She'd dropped a carrot at the news, and it rolled all the way under the table. "You named your tuba?"

"Why not?" he'd said. "People name spaceships all the time. Is a tuba that different?"

"From a spaceship? Yes. But also..." She'd been trying to rescue the carrot with her foot, but now she gave up and turned to him. "But also, you're *right*. Tubas deserve names."

It took her a couple days to come up with a name that felt right, but she nailed it.

"In honor of how it sings," she announced with a grin, "I'm calling it the Canary."

Later, for her birthday, he'd gotten the librarian to let him use the laminating machine, and made her a luggage tag with a yellow bird on it. She put it on her case immediately, beaming. "I don't think it's really a canary," he'd said apologetically. "I think it might be a parakeet or something."

"It's perfect. *And* hilarious."

Winston thought *she* was hilarious.

Also talented and smart and very pretty, and now he was having dramatic thoughts about her and, frankly, it was very confusing.

Thankfully, she didn't seem to notice. Instead, she cleared her throat and then said, "I'm going to tell you something, and I need you to act natural."

She hadn't even finished the sentence, and he was already sitting on the edge of his seat. "I've never acted more natural."

Frenchie nodded. "Great. Maybe also don't move your mouth when you talk."

"Like this?" he said, talking through his teeth and not moving his lips at all. It was harder than it looked.

"Perfect," she said, doing the same thing. "Now. What do you know about the criminal element?"

He spoke slowly. "Do you mean, do I know any criminals?" Then he pretended to take a bite out of his bologna sandwich, just for an excuse to move his mouth again.

"Sure," she said.

"Not *personally*," he said, talking as he fake-chewed. "But I've watched a lot of movies. What sort of criminal are you looking for?"

"I'm not *looking* for a criminal. I think I've *found* one. Actually, a bunch of them." She quickly scanned the cafeteria. "There's a criminal ring here at Subito."

"A criminal ring?" Winston asked, so surprised that he accidentally didn't disguise the question in any way.

"It's the teachers."

His jaw dropped.

"Look at them." She was very good at talking without moving her mouth. Winston wondered if she practiced it. "They've started wearing all black. Every one of them. That's weird, right? But okay, you say, maybe it's just a widespread fashion coincidence. Except also, they're having secret meetings after school. Almost every day. In the gym. The first time I noticed was by accident, and then I went back four times last week, pretending to wait for someone down the hall, and they go in, two or three at a time, but not casually, not *innocently. They look behind them before the door shuts.* To make sure they aren't being watched. They all do it." She paused.

"That *is* suspicious."

"I don't actually have any other evidence. Yet. So, what do you think?"

Winston took another fake bite of his sandwich while he thought. As he chewed, Frenchie nodded toward the center of the cafeteria. The two of them watched as Mr. DuBard, dressed all in black, slowly walked across the cafeteria, talking to himself. Directly in front of him, the kid who'd had the massive tray of milk cartons smashed one on his forehead, the milk spurting all over, and everyone around him squealing. DuBard walked right past, not even looking down, then spun in a complete circle, threw his hands up, and kept walking.

"He's brainwashed," Frenchie said. "That's a thing in organized crime."

"You know I want to believe you," Winston

began, "but... I've never seen the teachers be organized."

Frenchie was silent for a minute. "Fair. Just promise me that you'll pay attention."

✦

Over the next two periods, Winston watched carefully for signs that the teachers looked like criminals or that they were organized in any way. He watched as Mr. Colvin dropped a stapler and the staples fell out, scattering across the floor. He watched as Ms. Jardine cuddled the class hamster. He watched between classes, as teachers stood in their doorways and chatted happily with students.

And soon it was the last period of the day. Band.

Frenchie got there before him, so this time, he slid into place next to *her*, depositing the Lonesome carefully next to the Canary.

The band-and-orchestra room was too small for the number of kids crowded into it. The air clanged with the sound of metal music stands. There was a mural on one wall of the room, a giant piece of music, but instead of normal music notes, the round part at the bottom of each note was actually the head of a famous musician. Every note was a different musician, and each one had been painted by a different student from art class.

In the center, there was one extra-large music note, five feet high, made up of the smiling head of Yo-Yo Ma. Just above him was the definitely made-up quote:

When music called, I said, "CELLO!"

Winston loved the mural. He, too, felt that when music called, he had said, "Cello!"

Or more accurately, "Tuba!" but, well, that didn't make any sense.

At that moment, Mr. Manning was standing behind the podium at the front of the room while everyone got settled. He was tall and impossibly skinny, and in the same way that dogs and their owners sometimes look alike, it made a lot of sense that Mr. Manning played the bassoon.

The two tubas began pulling out their instruments.

"So?" Frenchie asked.

"I haven't seen anything suspicious," whispered Winston.

"And you've really been *looking*?" Frenchie asked.

"Of course I have," Winston said indignantly. "And I haven't seen a single suspicious thi—"

But he was interrupted by someone throwing the door open.

The band room went silent.

A woman he'd never seen before stood framed in the doorway. She looked over at Mr. Manning ominously. Winston couldn't put his finger on what *exactly* was ominous about it; it could have been the dark suit that was so out of place in school, or the sunglasses that made it impossible to see her eyes, or the clipboard she held so tightly that he could see her white knuckles from where he sat. Or it could have been *all* those things. He shrank down behind his music stand.

Everyone watched as the woman strode confidently over to Mr. Manning, pulled out a thick envelope, and handed it to him as she whispered something.

They just barely heard Mr. Manning reply, "I said only between classes."

The woman shrugged and walked out.

Mr. Manning stuffed the envelope under the huge stack of music on his podium. He glanced at the door, closing behind the woman, and wiped his brow.

Frenchie pulled Winston's T-shirt toward her, so their heads fit just behind the music stand. "We have to find out what's in that envelope," she whispered. "Stay here."

Winston opened his mouth and shut it.

He watched, unable to breathe, as she approached Mr. Manning with her tuba, asked him to look at a stuck valve and then put it on his chair so he had to turn away from the podium to inspect it. As he did, Frenchie scooted around behind him, as if she were getting a better view, but Winston saw her knock into the sheet music, pushing it around, before she said, "Oops! Sorry!"

Mr. Manning whirled around, holding the tuba, and just barely missed hitting her in the head. He looked at the stack of music in alarm and nearly bobbled the tuba as he handed it back. "This seems fine, Frenchie. I don't know what the problem was, but it's okay now!"

She was back at her seat in moments, a sly smile on her face.

"Success?" Winston whispered.

She raised her eyebrows. "It was full of money."

He gasped.

"And you know why she never took off the sunglasses?" she continued, speaking fast and keeping her voice low. *"So we can't identify her."*

The evidence was right there. Of...something. But that was definitely evidence.

It was hard to focus for the rest of class. Mr. Manning noticed. "Tubas, what is going on with you today? You keep rushing! It's like a prison break over there!"

They shot each other a look.

Why was Mr. Manning thinking about prisons?

By the time the bell rang Winston still hadn't come up with an answer that was anything other than bad news.

CHAPTER 3

THE COLD WATER in the second-floor girls' bathroom was the coldest water in the whole school. Louise Volpe splashed her face and then reached out for a paper towel.

Empty.

Great.

Since the last bell had rung and she was the only one in there, she squatted under the hand dryer to let the air blow-dry her cheeks, accidentally catching a glimpse of herself in the corner of the mirror.

Glimpses were the worst, even now, the way *every single time* her brain told her it might be her dad over there, and her heart edged toward her throat for that half second.

Being constantly ambushed by your own face?

Dumb.

She closed her eyes, feeling the air against her lashes. To be honest, she'd be fine if she never had to see her face ever again.

She'd have much preferred to look at her brain.

One hundred billion neurons, all doing their thing inside her head. That was the real Louise.

If she could only convince her brain to stop seeing her dad everywhere.

The sound of the door made her snap up to standing, and as the other girl walked in, Louise pretended to have been drying her hands. The girl took a stall, and this was irritating, because not only was Louise's face still damp, she'd been hoping for a few extra minutes alone. Whatever. She'd find another place. Swinging her backpack up, she headed off to the most important part of her day: Science Club.

Louise was the mastermind of Science Club. She was the one who had discovered that Dr. Omanid, her science teacher, arrived at school early and stayed at school late working on her own research. Louise was the one who convinced Dr. O to sponsor a club, crossing her heart that she wouldn't need any supervision at all.

"Cross your heart?" Dr. Omanid had asked, amused.

"I mean, I really, really promise not to need any supervision," Louise replied quickly, regretting her very unscientific turn of phrase.

But her begging had worked, and suddenly Louise had an excuse to spend as much time as possible in the school's chemistry lab. She had been the first, and for a while, the only member of Science Club.

Those were the days.

And it was almost like old times when she pushed the door to Dr. Omanid's classroom open a few minutes later. Totally quiet.

Perfect.

She headed straight for the supply closet, slipped inside, shut the door behind her, and turned off the light. The only sound was her own breath, and the supply closet was windowless, even better than the bathroom would have been because she could have absolute darkness. She'd been waiting for this moment all day.

So of course it only lasted a minute and a half.

The door flew open, and four pairs of glasses stared back at her.

She tried not to groan out loud.

Those glasses belonged to the four most irritating people in the world: the rest of Science Club.

"The Mad Scientist!" Tib Seneviratne exclaimed. This was Tib's favorite joke, because (as she loved telling Louise) she didn't mean *evil*, she meant angry, since Louise was always angry at something. Louise found it hard to argue with that logic. Looking angry all the time was, in fact, part of her strategy for being left alone. It never worked.

Tib had been the second person to join the club, and she was immediately so enthusiastic that the next time she'd gotten new glasses, she got frames with beakers in the corners. Now she stepped a foot into the supply closet and whispered conspiratorially, "Are you doing secret science in here?"

"No!" said Louise quickly. Too quickly, probably.

"Do you need help?" asked Eleni Bengle as she flipped on the light. Eleni was the smallest and the youngest—she'd skipped a grade on account of her weird superhuman memory, which *every* teacher absolutely *loved* to talk about. Her glasses were

100 percent bigger than her face, and seemed to make her especially effective at staring.

"Is this a closet-based experiment?" Vi Toro asked, looking around. She adjusted one of her Doctor Who suspenders, which she did when she was thinking hard. *Her* glasses were mustard yellow, to match the suspenders.

"I don't have a spreadsheet for closet-based experiments," Desirée Jones said. "I could *make* a spreadsheet, though. Why don't I make one?" She'd already pulled out her laptop. Desirée ran the numbers for all the club experiments (except Louise's). *She* had the kind of glasses that get dark in the sun and clear in low light.

Maybe they'll all just go away, Louise thought. She leaned, as boringly as possible, on a filing cabinet while she tried to think of something to say. "I'm . . . looking . . . for . . ." But she wasn't thinking of anything boring enough, and they did not go away.

Tragically.

Instead, they got even more interested. They crowded in, joining her in the closet and looking at her expectantly.

"What's next?" asked Vi.

"Should we shut the door?" asked Eleni.

"Shut the door!" cried Tib.

"I got it!" said Desirée as she slammed the door.

The four of them smiled at Louise.

I do not deserve this, she thought.

"Oh, turn the lights back off!" said Eleni.

"NO! I mean, no," Louise said. "It's okay. I was just...counting...supplies. Definitely no secret science going on in here." She tried to wiggle past them back toward the door, but her backpack caught on a shelf and she had to twist to slip it off and then unhook it. She squeezed between Tib and Vi and then put her hands on Eleni's shoulders and switched places with her so that she was now closer to the door. "Just counting supplies," she repeated casually.

"You were counting supplies with the lights off?" asked Eleni, looking up at her. Of course she'd pick up on that.

"You know I have a spreadsheet for supplies, right?" Desirée pointed out as Louise shimmied past her. "It's in the Science Club shared drive. You still haven't been able to access the drive?"

"Nope," Louise said.

She opened the door. Their positions were now completely reversed, with her outside the closet, looking in at the four of them. “Oops,” she said, and shut the door.

It wouldn’t hold them for long, but maybe they’d get distracted and discuss something. There was literally *nothing* they couldn’t turn into a two-hour discussion. After a year and a half of Science Club meetings, Louise felt like she knew everything about each of them, and frankly, she had better things to do with that brain space.

The problem was that she couldn’t walk away from Science Club. There were—and this was one of life’s great disappointments—not a lot of ways for an eleven-year-old to get access to a fully stocked chemistry laboratory.

So, for now, she was stuck with the four of them.

At the back of the classroom was the door to the shared chemistry lab—she headed straight there. Dr. Omanid was already inside, perched on her stool in one corner and typing relentlessly.

Dr. O waved but didn’t try talk, which only proved how great she was. She gave the people what they wanted.

The lab had three other entrances, from three

other classrooms, although Louise had never seen any other teacher in the dingy old room. This was Dr. O's domain. Shelves lined the walls, holding rows of identical bright green boxes. The five Science Club members each had their own box, in which they could keep the supplies they'd gotten with the skimpy Science Club money. Their own personal supplies for whatever they happened to be working on.

Louise, for example, was working on a cure for brain injuries.

Technically, Tib had been right. Louise *was* doing secret science. She had been for two years, even though it took time to get everything in place.

It started on the day of the press conference. Before it had all gone sour, there had been that player behind them, the one who asked for help. Winston stepped away to wave for the golf cart and she knelt down next to the man. He was clutching his leg. "Does it hurt?" she'd asked, like a dope. *Obviously it hurt.*

He'd growled.

"Win—*hurry*," she'd called over her shoulder to Winston, but he was too far away and the crowd was too loud and the wind was blowing and he seemed to be doing his best waving anyway. The man on the ground wearing a bear costume rolled slightly to one side and winced in pain. He was having trouble catching his breath.

Louise, desperate to do *some*thing, put her hand on his forehead, because that was all she could think to do. Slowly, his breath got steadier. "Thank you," he rasped.

"Did you break something?" she asked.

"Probably," he grunted. "I'm getting used to it."

Before she could stop herself, she was standing, her hands on her hips. "This happened *before*?"

He grimaced.

What about your daughter? she wanted to yell, but then of course, she had no idea if he had a daughter. She made her voice chilly. "Maybe you should stop."

"I can't stop," he said, and then laughed. Laughed! With a probably broken whatever! "This is what I'm *supposed* to do."

"Says who?" she muttered. "That's just dumb."

Still, she'd wiped the dirt off his face, the cart collected him, and she went back to stand with her family. A few moments later, the owner of the Chicago Horribles had made that joke, she headbutted him, and then, with his blood fresh in her hair, she suddenly and very clearly realized that the press conference was not going to bring her father back.

Why should it? It didn't change anything.

The only thing that could bring him back was a brain that wasn't totally disintegrating. And apparently, she was the only person who understood that. So she was going to have to make that happen herself.

That was what *she* was supposed to do.

Says me, she'd thought.

Within a few days, she started her search for a cure. She told exactly one person about it: Winston. He had blinked several times and then walked away, as if she'd never said anything at all. So she wasn't planning on telling anybody else, ever, not until she'd done it. Not until she'd found a cure.

But now she was getting close.

She knew it, in all of her hundred billion neurons. She knew because something had changed today.

Her work was finally paying off.

First, she'd turned her memories of her father into scientific lists: He had headaches all the time, he got confused about simple things, he needed sunglasses inside. He stood at the top of the stairs for hours, scared to walk down them. He wouldn't leave the house because he was afraid of getting lost, but walking was the only thing that made him feel better, so he paced.

He paced constantly.

So many of her early memories were from sitting at the foot of the stairs and watching him do laps around the house. He joked about it back then—called himself Pac-Man, and one time even told her that ghosts were chasing him. That was before he got too broken to joke, and she did not include that particular memory in the official list of observations, because she'd started crying about the ghosts and he'd held her and apologized—it was a bad joke, he said—and she remembered the feeling of being held by him, but in the end, the memory was just too complicated for science.

She also did her research—Louise read all about brains. About how brains were like three pounds of perfectly orchestrated electrical storms. About how her dad's type of broken brain was the result of being hit in the head so many times that now his brain cells were shorting out, their electricity spitting off in the wrong directions. How once it started, it just got worse and worse.

And the only thing that could stop it was oxygen.

Of course there was a catch. Cells needed oxygen to heal, but if they had too much, it was useless, like filling up a glass of water until it overflowed. You weren't going to get any more water in the glass no matter how hard you tried.

Human cells could only eat so much oxygen, and it wasn't enough.

That was where Louise hit a wall. She kept reading, at school, online, at the library, but the wall of science seemed impenetrable.

And then, as chance would have it, the sixth grade went on a field trip to the aquarium. She realized, all at once, that she'd been stuck on humans. Now, right in front of her, there was a four-and-a-half-legged starfish in the shallow pool, and a description on the wall of how the starfish could regenerate that leg! There was the sea cucumber, who could repair its own organs! And finally, there was the jellyfish.

Her heart started beating faster, sending her own brain more oxygen as she stood before a wall of glowing blobs, reading about them on their own small plaque.

Jellyfish could live deep, deep in the ocean, where

there wasn't much oxygen. Jellyfish were very, very clever about oxygen—they could store it for when they needed it. They were also very good at healing. They could build their entire bodies back if they had to.

This is it, she'd thought.

Jellyfish knew how to make the glass bigger.

Humans needed to be more like jellyfish. If they could do that, if they could just make the glass bigger, they could heal their own brains.

She went back to Science Club dizzy with excitement. The order form for chemicals was simple. Louise carefully put a check mark beside the chemicals she wanted—fluorescent proteins like the ones in jellyfish—and when Dr. O gave her the box two weeks later, Louise's hands shook.

She mixed and matched, swirling together a little from this jar and a little from that one. The results were labeled *G.L.O.P.* (Greater Levels of Oxygen Project) and assigned a number.

She tested each version of G.L.O.P. on a small spot on her hand. If there was no bad reaction, the next day, she put it on her whole hand and then examined the skin under the microscope.

Conveniently, it looked like she was trying to make hand lotion.

Louise wrote down her observations in a notebook that she kept with her supplies. She had not observed anything remarkable until yesterday, when she noticed a change that she didn't understand. She went all in, covering her arms and face with G.L.O.P. #17. As of five minutes ago in the supply closet, the results were consistent.

Before she could have conclusions, Louise knew that she would have to get the same results over and over again. That was the key, because science had to be, among other things, reliable.

That was one of the nicest things about science as far as Louise was concerned.

She grabbed her bright green box and brought it to her favorite table, the opposite corner from Dr. O, the table where she'd sat when it had just been the two of them. It was a good table, because she had a view of the whole room and nobody could sneak up on her and ask if she needed help.

The rest of Science Club absolutely *loved* offering to help. It was like a contagion.

Just then, Tib's voice drifted into the lab. "I'm pretty sure she's back here."

Louise tried to ignore the others as they walked in, but something made her look up. A woman wearing a dark suit and sunglasses followed Tib into the lab. *Why the sunglasses?* Louise thought. She appreciated protective eye gear when it was necessary, but this was hardly the moment. The woman stepped up to Dr. O, and the two of them spoke in low tones as they looked over something on the woman's clipboard.

Louise lost interest and returned to her work.

On the table in front of her, she carefully organized her tools. A microscope. Slides. The delicate jars, carefully labeled, with all the chemical compounds that Dr. Omanid had ordered for her.

There were also seventeen slightly smaller ones, the mixing jars. She flipped open the lid to G.L.O.P. #17.

This was the one that she was excited about.

With a tiny spatula, she spread some G.L.O.P. on a slide and then carefully put the top slide on, sandwiching the goo inside.

Then she found the slide she'd made from the same jar the day before. She compared the two slides under the microscope.

Since yesterday, the solution had not changed at all. No separating like old salad dressing. No turning a different color. No smell.

A shiver of excitement ran up her spine.

If this was how mad scientists felt, Louise was okay being called a mad scientist.

Because before the Science Club members had thrown open the closet door, flooding the small room with light, she'd had just enough time. She hadn't been able to see her face, but she'd looked down at her arms, there in the pitch-black among the supplies.

Her arms, hands, fingers—they glowed.

Like a jellyfish.

The G.L.O.P. was working.

CHAPTER 4

WINSTON MADE THE five-block walk to school by himself, replaying over and over again the moment of Mr. Manning accepting the envelope from the mysterious woman.

The walk was quiet, since Louise had left early. Like every day so far this year.

Science Club.

Winston'd asked her about it once, what she did there, but she said she was finding a cure for brain damage, and he didn't understand why she'd make such a mean joke, just to keep him from knowing what she was doing, so he'd shut up about it.

As soon as he got to school, he waded through

the groups of kids until he found Frenchie. She was leaning against the building, her tuba case by her feet, looking exceptionally cool. And also pretty calm for someone who had probably just uncovered a massive conspiracy.

He leaned against the wall beside her, putting down the Lonesome.

But the grass wasn't even and the Lonesome tilted, so now his tuba case was resting against Frenchie's and he was more aware of it than he'd ever been before in the entire time they'd known each other. Surely their tubas had leaned against each other before.

Why was he turning into a total weirdo?

And how could he stop it?

"What are we going to do? About the teachers, I mean," he said quickly. If he was lucky, she'd think it was the teacher conspiracy causing these random blushing attacks. "I'm not good with my face. They're going to take one look at me and know that I know."

"Maybe—but I don't think so. They're used to being the top of the food chain. They think they're too sneaky to be caught," she said, twisting the end of her ponytail. "If we're going to catch them, we'll need proof."

"If we're going to *what* now—"

"We'll need more than the woman in the suit," Frenchie mused. "We'll need to follow the money."

"Follow the—why do we need proof?"

Frenchie gave him a sideways look. "We have to stop them."

"Do we?" Winston squeaked. He turned to her, almost tripping over the two tuba cases. "I don't think that's the best use of us. We can't stop them. We're not some sort of, I don't know, organized rebel force, for example, and you need organization to take down an organization—we aren't *organized*—and I *do not have the face for this*—"

"You have to stop saying 'organize,'" Frenchie said firmly. "Winston, we have a responsibility here. We need to find out what sort of criminals they are. Like, are they endangering students? Are they embezzling money from the school board?"

"Interplanetary power consolidation?" he whispered.

"What?"

"Never mind."

"And once we know what's going on, then we decide what to do with the information," she finished.

"Why does it have to be *us*?" Winston slid down the wall, putting his head between his knees. He really would have preferred to spend the rest of eternity avoiding his teachers.

"We're the ones who know," Frenchie said simply.

"And depending on what it is, maybe we do nothing?"

"Sure," Frenchie said, utterly unconvincingly.

Not one tiny little piece of him believed that she'd drop it if she got solid evidence against the teachers.

But this was Frenchie.

He'd known her since first grade, known her a little, the way you know somebody who never sits at the same table with you in any class. He didn't start to *really* know her until they ended up sitting next to each other in band, holding nearly identical tubas with no idea how to play them.

If the tuba brought them together, it was the Horribles that made them friends.

After that unlikely win at the press conference game, the Chicago Horribles won a couple of *more* games, *in a row*. It was a miracle. The city was in shock. People dressed in Chicago Horribles shirts, hats, scarves, socks, whispering about the possibility that this might be The Year. Someone—probably someone else's dad, a dad who had *not* disappeared—pointed out that maybe Lenny Volpe had been the bad luck the whole time.

That when he vanished, so did the losing streak.

That *he* was the curse.

Not that winning a few games actually changed that much in the end. They were still the worst team in the league. But it was under Lenny Volpe that they'd started losing—and they just hadn't ever stopped. Until now. Now Chicago had hope, and it was making them mean.

The infamous quarterback had retired when Winston was six, so it wasn't until the vanishing that Winston understood how much the city had hated his dad. He learned that people had taken out personal ads in the newspaper to get his dad removed from the team. That there had been entire talk shows dedicated to the mistakes he'd made..And once he was gone, the city didn't rally to find him. The press conference never stood a chance.

Instead, Lenny Volpe became a punch line to a joke about how the football team could finally win a few games.

Winston didn't understand how the worst thing

that had ever happened to him only made people want to joke around. He walked through the halls of Subito, hearing the word *curse* whispered by lockers, imagining that he could play the tuba all the time and drown everyone out.

Drown out everyone except Frenchie.

Frenchie never made fun of his dad.

When the trumpet section couldn't stop giggling about it during band one day, Frenchie shut them down with a look so ferocious Winston was surprised they were even able to walk later. She started finding him between classes and talked extra loud if they heard somebody mention the Volpe Curse. She'd even tripped a few people who, honestly, totally deserved it.

Frenchie was the best human he knew.

So if she wanted him to do something? It wasn't like he'd ever say no.

✦

The first bell rang, and they walked to the band room to drop off their tubas, trying to avoid teachers and not get trampled by other students, while Frenchie told him the plan.

"We start with that envelope."

"The enormous envelope of mysterious money that we will probably never see again?"

She nodded, not getting his point.

It didn't help that just then, a new wave of kids from the side entrance flowed past them, knocking Winston's case into Frenchie's. They were used to it—pushing through the hallways with the big cases was always a little like being inside a pinball machine—but it was *not* the ideal time to hatch a plan.

They got to the band room door and stepped inside—Mr. Manning wasn't there.

"Perfect," Frenchie whispered as she dropped her case. "Can you put this away for me?" She was already halfway across the room, faster without the tuba, heading straight toward the little office at the back. It was where Mr. Manning kept all the sheet music files—but he also had a small desk in there.

Frenchie disappeared inside.

Winston lugged the Lonesome over to the cabinet and put it in. He'd just gotten back to the Canary when the door opened.

Crap.

Mr. Manning.

"Mr. Manning!" Winston said loudly. "Oh, wow, it's you!"

Mr. Manning, because he was Mr. Manning, did not seem to think this was suspicious. Instead, he bowed.

Winston's mind raced. He needed to get Mr. Manning out of the room. Also he needed to fix his face. His face was definitely saying too many things right now. Probably all of them were going to get Frenchie caught.

His face or Mr. Manning.

Which one should he fix first?

"That's not your tuba, is it?" Mr. Manning asked, pointing at Frenchie's case with the canary luggage tag.

Winston froze.

Then he wasn't even a little worried about his face anymore, the real problem was his heartbeat, booming out of his chest, louder than the loudest drum in all of Subito's percussion line, the timpani, and he hoped Mr. Manning couldn't feel the beat through the floor like you could when the timpani played, that he wasn't giving himself away, that he was going to give away—

"No, it's mine, Mr. Manning," Frenchie said next to him suddenly.

"Oh, hello, Frenchie! I didn't see you there!"

"Probably because I was being sneaky!"

They both laughed.

Winston did not. He closed his eyes. He wasn't cut out for this stuff. He wasn't a spy. He wasn't a rebel force.

"Winston's still a little sleepy," Frenchie explained, like him freaking out was no big deal. She nudged him. "Winston? I don't want to miss the second bell."

He reluctantly opened his eyes to see Frenchie and Mr. Manning staring at him, and before he could say anything else incriminating, Frenchie grabbed his sleeve and pulled him out into the hallway.

"Have a musical day!" Mr. Manning called after them from the doorway.

The moment they were out of earshot, Winston whispered, "I can't do this. I almost got you caught. It's not going to work."

"But it *did* work," Frenchie said, beaming. "I figured out what the money's for."

Winston's timpani of a heart held still.

"There was a notebook on his desk, like an accounting book, just lying open. There was only one entry. 'Cash, $300, Tails.'"

"'Cash, $300, Tails.'"

"That was it."

"Tails, like..."

"The only thing I can think of is the kind of tail who follows somebody."

Winston tried to put it together. "The woman in the suit paid them to tail somebody?"

Frenchie nodded. "And there's one other weird thing. I didn't get to do any other poking around, but I did pick up the notebook, and I saw what was on the cover. He'd written a name."

The hairs on Winston's arms stood up.

"Brian Dolph."

The hairs sat back down. "*Brian Dolph?* That doesn't make any sense. You're sure?"

She nodded.

They both had language arts first period, but with different teachers, so once they arrived, they stood just outside the rooms, waiting until the last minute, like maybe they were more powerful together, and somehow they might come up with the answer. They both thought as hard as possible.

The bell rang, though, before the answer came, and they slipped into their classrooms. Winston forgot to worry about his face, because he was so preoccupied with the mystery of Brian Dolph.

Brian Dolph was in the grade just above them.

He was a boring bully, unexceptional, except for one sort of dramatic detail.

The copy machine incident.

Everyone knew about the copy machine incident. It was impossible not to.

Last year, Brian Dolph had gotten detention. He was offered the option of cleaning out an old closet in the main office. He took it.

The job required digging through a box that held every instruction manual for every piece of equipment the school had bought in the last thirty years—the box was bursting with useless directions for machines that no longer existed. He was asked to make two piles: the equipment that was still used and the equipment that had been replaced. He had a list to use as reference.

Among the manuals, Brian Dolph discovered one for the current copy machine.

That manual did not make it into a pile.

Several weeks later, after having brought the manual home and reading it carefully, Brian Dolph got the opportunity he'd been looking for when the school had a routine fire drill.

As everyone else left the building, he slipped into the office. With no one around, he changed the settings for the copier, making it so every single copy printed with the same back page. It was the sort of setting that a school might use to put their name and logo on the back of every document.

In the end, it was clear that Brian Dolph did not think through the prank. When his copier-smushed face appeared on the back of every single test and worksheet, he couldn't exactly deny that he'd done it. Faced with the evidence, he claimed that he couldn't remember how to change it back.

Whether he remembered, Brian Dolph had jammed it, for real, bad enough that the repairman they hired couldn't figure out how to un-jam it.

Later, Brian explained to anyone who would listen that, as a graduating eighth grader, he'd already been on the lookout for the perfect prank, and that detention fell in his lap like a gift. Overnight, Brian Dolph became a legend.

And so even though he was now in high school, Brian's smushed face continued to haunt the pages of Subito's worksheets, tests, and handouts.

What did it mean that he was somehow involved? Why were the teachers tailing *him*? None of it fit together.

Not in any way that Winston could see, at least.

But somehow, he just *knew*, it *did* fit together. He half ignored the class going on around him, instead thinking about Brian Dolph and the smushed face and the teachers.

For two years, his life had revolved around one awful, unsolvable mystery. Now, right in front of him, was a mystery he could do something about.

He wanted to solve this mystery with every bone in his body.

Ms. Avila called on him.

He looked up, meeting the language arts teacher's eyes.

He was perfectly in control of his face. His face was just fine.

CHAPTER 5

ON SUNDAY EVENING, Louise came home from the library to find a note from her mom sliding down the front of the refrigerator and Winston asleep on the sofa in front of a football game.

Specifically, a Chicago Horribles game.

In the days right after the disappearance, he'd told her that he didn't actually watch the games, he just liked falling asleep to the sound. Whenever she found him like that now, she turned off the game, and by the time he woke up and went to bed, she was already asleep.

But tonight was different.

Louise couldn't find the remote.

She looked around quietly, but it wasn't anywhere. Winston muttered something in his sleep. *Ugh,* she thought. Was it *under* him? She didn't like hearing the sounds of the game float through the house, but she wasn't going to move him and risk waking him up. There had to be a button on the actual TV somewhere, so she stepped up to it and felt around the hard plastic edges.

And that was how she got close enough to see something she never would have seen otherwise.

There was a *bear* on the field.

In a cage.

She didn't believe it at first, so she'd leaned in, inches away from the screen. It wasn't one of the players, joking around. There was an actual bear on the field.

She stood in front of the TV for the whole second half, watching, unable to tear her eyes away. The camera never landed squarely on it, but it kept appearing in the corners of the screen, and she could see the shape of the bear inside.

The bear couldn't stay still.

It was pacing.

Her stomach turned.

She was instantly back at the bottom of the stairs,

sucked into the memory of watching her dad pass her again and again, going nowhere. She pressed her forehead against the screen.

Somebody has to get that bear out of there, she thought.

✦

She'd tried to sleep, but by 3:30 the next morning, Louise was still wide awake and couldn't stop thinking about the bear.

From all her research, she knew that there were some kinds of spiders that were 80 percent brain; as in, they had so many brains that their brains filled their whole bodies and went down into their legs, and that was how Louise felt, lying in bed, unable to get back to sleep. Like she had brains all the way down to her legs.

Why fight it? she decided.

She got out of bed and dressed, pulling on jeans and a blue hoodie.

Without any real sort of plan, she walked through the quiet house.

She opened the front door and stared out onto the block. Even the birds weren't awake yet. Everything was so *quiet*. But she supposed it made sense.

Most adults were still asleep. They weren't taking up space yet.

And that meant Louise could do whatever she wanted.

She shut the door quietly—it would ruin everything if she woke up her mom or Winston—and walked toward the back of the house, grabbing her helmet on the way. In the kitchen, she scribbled out a note about super-early Science Club, put it under a magnet that immediately slipped a few inches down the fridge, and left through the back door. She rolled her bike down the narrow passageway between her house and next door, out to the street, and then hopped on. Out of habit, she turned her light on, but she probably didn't need it.

In the dark morning, she was still glowing.

She pedaled on.

She pedaled along her block, where the small houses stood shoulder to shoulder, thin spaces between them. She pedaled past the tangle of bridges that ran overhead. She pedaled past the police station, crossing her fingers against her handlebar that no one noticed her. She pedaled past the historic houses, lights in their gardens. She pedaled onto the ramp that would switch back and take her over the train yards.

Below her, the trains sat empty and waiting.

As she turned onto the down ramp, she started picking up speed, the sharp air feeling good against her face.

A few minutes later, she was at the stadium.

It sat along the edge of Lake Michigan, hulking and out of place—halfway on land, halfway on the water, like a giant ship somebody had run into the ground.

A ship with a bear somewhere inside.

Louise stopped a few yards away, one foot on the ground, unsure for a second. It was no use pretending she hadn't come here to help the bear. But what could she actually *do*?

With that question in mind, she locked up her bike and began walking around the stadium. After going a few minutes in one direction, she noticed movement—an old man without a shirt, running up and down the outer stadium stairs with weights in his hands. She stopped. For some reason, she was glad to see him, whoever he was—maybe it was just nice to know that she wasn't alone out there. Even so, she turned and walked in the opposite direction, toward the water.

When she got to the place where the building

jutted out over the lake, she had to climb over rocks to keep going, but it wasn't an impossible climb, and halfway across, she discovered a hidden dock where boats could pull up. It was right outside the door of a glass-walled room that looked out onto the water. At first, she peered in, her face pressed to the huge windows, but then, feeling reckless, she tried the door.

It was open.

Someone had forgotten to lock it.

So she stepped inside.

The room echoed with growls.

She almost ran right back out, but instead, she forced herself to stand still. Willed her heart to slow back down. *It isn't real,* she told herself.

The recording—because it *was* a recording, it was *definitely* a recording, playing to nobody in that strange round room—the recording was doing a very good job of sounding like a bear.

Louise'd been in the stadium a few times, walking around the maze of offices and locker rooms with her dad while he proudly introduced her to people. That was before he disappeared, before the press conference, and a lot had happened since then, but she didn't ever remember being in this room.

And this wasn't the kind of room you'd forget.

She took a few more steps toward the center, trying to understand. Something was happening in there, something very *on purpose.* It made her think of bears, even aside from the soundtrack, and as she slowly turned, she suddenly understood why.

The floor was shaped like a bear's paw.

A giant open paw.

Opposite the glass walls, there were five doors. One for each finger. Did bears *have* fingers? Or were they called something else? She'd find out.

But she knew that's what they were because on top each of the five doors, a razor-sharp metal blade sliced into the wall and ran up toward the ceiling, where it edged into a deadly point. Those were definitely claws.

A shiver ran up her spine.

She was standing right in the palm of a bear paw.

And it looked like it had been forgotten—the room had spiderwebs and dust where the curving walls met the floor. At the very least, it had been a while since the room had been cleaned.

Four of the doors on the far side of the room were labeled *Hibernator Suite* and numbered. She opened Hibernator Suite No. 1 and discovered a perfect sort of cabin inside, the kind she imagined might exist on ships, complete with a cozy-looking bed. The other three were the same, although it was clear no one had used them for a long time.

The fifth door—the thumb?—opened onto a hallway. That must be where the room connected to the rest of the stadium. She glanced back, and on the other side of the wide glass walls, the lake sat, dark and calm. She could leave now and head home.

Or she could keep going.

For the next hour, she snuck through dark halls of the stadium, learning the twists and turns of the place and trying to find the bear. The only people in the whole place were hanging out in what looked like a guard station, and she could see them through windows drinking coffee and laughing with each other. She crept past it easily. They didn't expect anyone, so they weren't looking.

She poked her nose into every single room—she even looked out onto the field, which she'd been hoping to avoid, although when she finally saw it with the security lights on, it looked weird and fake and small, more like the deserted part of the mall than how she'd seen it two years ago. And anyway, it was completely bear-free. Not even worth it.

But she still had a problem: The bear wasn't

anywhere, and if she couldn't *find* it, she couldn't *help* it. Louise headed back to the bear paw room, frustrated. She wanted to kick something.

That would just make her foot hurt, though.

What *would* make her feel better?

Revenge.

First, she paid a return visit to a vast, junk-filled area she'd found not too far away from the bear room. She quickly found what she was looking for—a rolling cart that would save her a lot of time—then, as she was leaving, a can of silver spray paint winked at her from the corner.

Yes, please, she thought.

And then she went to the equipment room, loaded up the cart, and, one batch at a time, wheeled the Chicago Horribles' helmets down the hall to the closest open window and threw them into Lake Michigan. When she was done, she spray-painted a giant *V* for *Volpe* where the helmets had been and, with a bounce in her step, returned the cart to the junk room. After a moment of deliberation, she kept the spray paint.

It was dawn by the time she got back to the bear room—the sun was beginning to rise over the lake. She stared out at the pink-and-gold sky pouring itself across the surface of the water. The effect was so beautiful that a less-scientific person could almost forget it was the result of the light bending through pollution.

It was tricky how sometimes things could be right and wrong at the same time.

And then she snuck out the way she'd come, over the rocks and to her bike, which carried her home just in time to see the back of her mom's car drive away.

She ate a quick bologna breakfast and left for school, dragging herself through the day, and so exhausted by the time she walked into the lab after the final bell that it took her a second to realize that something was horribly wrong.

"WHAT IS THAT NOISE?" she demanded from the doorway.

The four other members of Science Club spun around from their various workstations, huge smiles across their faces.

"It's music?" Eleni said helpfully. She pointed to the computer against the wall where the song blared from the speakers.

Kitten takes a bath, now she does her civic duty
Chases lasers all day long
Then she votes and shakes that booty

What.

Louise had taken too long to get to the lab. She'd stopped off at her locker, and that was clearly a mistake. Big mistake.

Meow, meow, go run for public office
Meow, meow, let's talk about the caucus

Biggest mistake ever. She was never going to be late to Science Club again.

Then she realized Eleni was giving her a weird look. "You were joking, though, right?" Eleni asked. "You *do* know Kittentown Dynamo?"

Louise shook her head approximately one millimeter.

There was a collective gasp in the room.

"You don't know Kittentown Dynamo?" Vi burst incredulously. She was wearing protective goggles over her glasses, which was making her seem double incredulous, if such a thing was possible.

"This album is her masterpiece," Tib said breathlessly. "*Good Kittizenship.*"

"Get it?" asked Vi. "Like 'good *citizen*ship'? But with kittens."

Louise thought she might die of whatever the opposite of science was.

"I'm so jealous," said Desirée, sighing. "I wish I could hear it for the first time again."

"This album is going to *change your life*," Vi exclaimed confidently.

"I don't *need* to change my life," Louise said. "My life is fine." She stomped over to her usual spot, dropped her backpack, and grabbed her box from the shelves before she had time to think too hard about whether her life really was fine. Anyway, it didn't matter. She was absolutely certain that whatever her life might need, it wasn't a pop star named Kittentown Dynamo.

Also, that was a dumb name.

She'd gotten her workstation ready by the time the song ended, and when the computer rolled into the next song, she looked up. "We have to listen to another one?"

The other members of the club, each of them at their different tables, bent over Bunsen burners and beakers, quietly singing along with Kittentown Dynamo, turned their big, glasses-wearing puppy dog eyes toward Dr. O.

Louise was certain that Dr. O would side with her, but instead, she just gave them all a bemused look over her reading glasses. "It's your job to govern yourselves," she said, shrugging. "I'm just here for the occasional scientific oversight."

"Club meeting!" called Tib.

"Yay!" said the other three.

Louise put her head down on the table. What had she done.

"Middle table!" said Tib as they all gathered, like moths to a Bunsen burner flame.

"I'll take notes!" volunteered Desirée.

"I'll get snacks!" said Vi, pulling out a bag of Jelly Babies she kept in her bag for special occasions. What Vi considered special was not what Louise considered special.

"I'll find the meetingest-y song!" chirped Eleni, already at the computer.

"And I'll *pass*," Louise said, scribbling in her notebook.

"But... you're the one who suggested it in the first place," said Tib.

"Incorrect," Louise said. "I didn't ask for a meeting. Also, I have science to do."

"You can wait for five minutes," said Tib. "And you *did* want to talk about the music situation."

Louise looked at them all staring at her.

"Fine," she huffed. If only Science Club weren't such a democracy.

"I'd like to call this meeting to order," said Tib.

"Order," said the other four in unison.

"Desirée," Tib began the meeting. "How long since our last official meeting?"

"Two weeks," said Desirée, pushing up her glasses.

"All right. First order of business: playing music during lab time. Thoughts?"

"I think it's distracting," said Louise.

"Other opinions?" asked Tib thoughtfully.

"I love it," said Eleni.

"Very helpful," said Vi.

"Fun," said Desirée.

"Science Club isn't supposed to be *fun*," said Louise. They other four stared at her. "What?"

"It sort of is," said Tib.

"Ugh," said Louise.

Eleni raised her hand. "How about we say each member of Science Club gets to have a day where they pick the music? Or"—she nodded to Louise—"the *non*-music? That covers all five days of the week."

Louise groaned, but the sound was drowned out by the unanimous votes of the others.

Tib declared the matter settled. "Now, why don't we do a check-in?" Check-ins were a waste of time, but Tib loved them. The four of them went through their experiments with Louise barely paying attention, and finally, they all turned to her.

She shrugged. "Same as usual."

"You're..." Eleni was definitely trying to sound positive. "Still working on hand lotion?"

Louise nodded.

"Do you...think you're getting any closer?" asked Vi tentatively.

"Yeah, probably," said Louise.

"Um, good," said Tib.

"Way to persevere," added Eleni.

"Thanks," Louise said. "Meeting adjourned?"

"Meeting adjourned," said Tib sadly.

"Adjourned," the other three said in unison.

Louise, trying to block out the steady stream of Kittentown Dynamo, returned to her workstation. She had actual work to do. She made a new slide and once again compared the slides dated from the previous few days.

She frowned.

This time, there was a difference between the new slide and the previous one. G.L.O.P. #17 was getting watery.

That was no good. An unstable solution wasn't going to be taken seriously. Louise needed it to be stable. Reliable. She chewed on her lip, then turned to a new page in the notebook to write down her findings. At the top of each page was a jellyfish. It wasn't a proper, scientific drawing of a jellyfish, but she liked it.

It reminded her that she was doing exactly what she was supposed to be doing. And that was how she'd get her dad back.

Meanwhile, across town, someone else thought Lenny Volpe had *already* come back.

CHAPTER 6

THE MAN WAS wearing a bear costume, and the problem was that as he ran, the head part kept flopping down over his eyes so that he couldn't see clearly. It meant that periodically, he stumbled into the walls along the hallway, an inconvenience that might have stopped anyone else. But this man was a football player, and he was used to that sort of thing, so he just kept running.

The head of security for the Chicago Horribles, Tybalt Rawls, was watching this happen on the security camera screens mounted along the wall in his office.

The man dressed like a bear had darted out of the

equipment room, moving from one of Rawls's black-and-white screens to another as he tore through the locker room, down the players' hall, turning onto the coaches' hall, and then all the way to the security office, where he barged in, suddenly appearing in front of Rawls in real life, tripping over a chair in the middle of the office that he hadn't seen because of the hood of the bear costume, and somersaulting himself all the way to the foot of the desk.

The head of security sighed.

The man in the bear costume, who'd had the wind knocked out of him, stood up too fast, and immediately got dizzy.

"Head between your legs," Rawls commanded.

The man followed instructions. "Ohst oblem," he mumbled once he was in position. The words, coming from both under the bear hood *and* between his legs, were muffled.

"Hm?" Rawls asked impatiently.

The man, risking a new wave of dizziness, looked up. "We . . . we got a ghost problem."

Rawls must have heard wrong. "What kind of problem?"

"It took all the helmets."

"*What* took all the helmets?"

"There's a *ghost*. And it took all the dang helmets."

Seconds later, they were charging back to the equipment room, the head of security leading the way with a grim look on his face.

They burst into the locker room to find the rest of the team standing around in their own droopy bear costumes. Rawls didn't break his stride as he noted that not a single helmet hung from any of the lockers. He plowed onward to the equipment room, where he brushed aside several players who'd been grouped by the door, staring.

Usually, the equipment room was like a library of all things football, with shelves and shelves of shoes, shoulder pads, mouth guards, extra uniforms, helmets; whatever your football-playing heart desired, it could be found that room.

Rawls used to love that room. He'd loved it way back when he'd started his career as a part-time weekend guard, just out of high school. During the quiet moments back then, he'd sit in the equipment room under the guise of helping polish helmets and think about all that safety. About a whole room dedicated to the careful protecting of a body. His life, which had felt unpredictable to that point, was desperate for such a room.

So he had stayed, working his way up in the job of making-people-safe, steadily, from part-time night guard to head of security.

The longer he stayed, the less he believed it was possible to keep anybody safe.

And now, like a final kick in the pants, some ghost had gone and burgled the room that started it all.

The shelves were full all around the great room, except for the ones that once held the helmets. They'd been stripped clean, so that the room now resembled a great mouth with missing teeth.

And right in the middle of the floor was a giant silver *V*.

The man who'd run all the way to his office whispered just at his shoulder. "See that *V*? It's the ghost of Lenny Volpe."

At the mention of the former quarterback, Rawls sucked in a breath.

"It's the ghost of Lenny Volpe," the man repeated, "and he has unfinished business. Probably because we said he was a curse."

"That's not a *V*—it's a Roman numeral five," said another player.

"Lenny Volpe played number five," argued someone else.

"That's what I'm saying—it's a five, for Lenny Volpe," the man clarified.

"So we're all in agreement here, though: It's definitely the ghost of Lenny Volpe," said the original runner.

The men murmured.

"*No*," said Rawls firmly. "There's no such thing as ghosts."

"But look..." The man waved over another player, who reluctantly handed him a phone. "Jerry and Kaz, they've been pranking each other all season, where they do stuff to each other's uniforms—"

Rawls rubbed his temples. That better not be a migraine coming on.

"*And anyway*, Kaz set up a trap to take a picture of what Jerry was going to do so he wouldn't be surprised, but look what he caught instead."

He held up the phone, and the head of security squinted at the image.

There was, unmistakably, a blurry glowing bluish blob.

"It's the ghost of Lenny Volpe," said the man breathlessly.

"It's not." The head of security did not disguise his irritation. "It's just a very bad picture."

The players murmured. It was clear that they disagreed with him. "What about the *V*?" the man asked.

"You mean the five?" somebody else said.

Lenny Volpe had worn the number five. That part was inarguably true. The rest of it was superstition. This, Rawls thought with chagrin, was what happened when you had a team that kept losing. They started to lean on good luck, bad luck, curses, all those other explanations for what was, in truth, just bad playing. It was just too tempting to not accept responsibility for your own mistakes. But he wasn't the coach, so it wasn't his place to suggest that the players change their perspective.

He sighed. "Ghosts do not use spray paint."

The man thought that over. "You think, what, they'd use ectoplasm, or some such?"

The head of security didn't answer. He just stared at the empty shelves where the helmets had been.

The man continued. "Okay, sure, but what about if you have a more cleanliness-oriented ghost? Like maybe spray paint was simpler than getting all gooey, you know?"

The head of security turned around to address the team. "This is not a supernatural situation. This is simple theft and vandalism. And we will figure out who did it." He glanced across the players. The uniforms had been specifically designed to fit over the helmets, and without them, the players looked like teddy bears with the stuffing pulled out of the top. "You probably need to worry about finding some new helmets."

He stalked out, listening to the whispers behind him. They were still convinced it was a ghost. Bunch of superstitious ninnies.

Rawls didn't believe in ghosts. He believed that when you died, you died dead. You didn't die just to have to fool around with unfinished business. You finished your business the moment you kicked it.

Still, it had thrown him when they brought Lenny Volpe into it.

He generally didn't know individual players that well, but when the anti–Lenny Volpe groups got vicious, he'd been assigned to be security for the guy. He had expected the man to be a diva, but he wasn't, not by a long shot. Volpe was funny and nice, and one time, he'd told Rawls that if the crowd ever got rough, he should just get out of there and make sure he didn't get hurt. "I'll be fine," Volpe had said reassuringly.

Of course, he hadn't been fine.

Back in his office, Rawls sent a quick memo to all the guard staff, and then he pulled up the overnight footage of the locker room area.

He sped through the hours of stillness until finally, finally, there was some movement. Then he slowed it down to normal playback and watched as the helmets were stolen, slowly, deliberately, one at a time taken off the shelf and walked off camera into the locker room.

His mouth had fallen open, though he didn't realize it.

He didn't believe in ghosts.

Not ectoplasmic ones or any other kind.

But there on the screen, very clearly, a ghost was methodically stealing the helmets of the Chicago Horribles. That ghost was burgling him cold.

It was a blue-white blob and it glowed almost translucent, in a way that the other photo hadn't quite captured. And there was no way around it: The blob resembled Lenny Volpe. The shape of the face. The hair. Those shoulders.

He couldn't take this to the police.

He'd watched the footage three times when he was startled out of it by one of the regular guards popping into his doorframe.

"We got 'em."

"You—what?" The head of security paused the video. "You got what?" An image sprang into his mind: the ghost, being handcuffed and led away, ashamed of its actions. Could you handcuff a ghost?

"The helmets, sir? We got the helmets."

For the second time that morning, the head of security sprang out of his chair and raced through the hallways of the stadium. This time, instead of going down, into the players' territory, they went up, past the front offices and into the elevator that took them to the very top of the stadium. The west side faced the city, but the east side looked out onto the wide expanse of a perfectly aquamarine-colored Lake Michigan. And from there, he saw what exactly had become of the helmets.

If he'd been near the ocean, he might have thought they were seals.

Down below, a couple hundred helmets bobbed calmly in the gentle lake current.

Maybe it *was* Lenny Volpe.

Maybe he was back.

CHAPTER 7

WINSTON LOOKED AT himself in the mirror.

Was the trench coat too much?

He couldn't tell.

Now that he'd turned on his inner detective, it was impossible to turn off. Winston struck a pose, looking over his shoulder. *He wanted answers and he wanted them yesterday.* He frowned.

Yesterday morning, if at all possible.

Since that day in the cafeteria, Winston hadn't been able to think about anything other than the mystery surrounding the teachers. So the fact that it took him and Frenchie three whole days to find anyone who knew where Brian Dolph lived was straight-up torture. When Frenchie finally called to say that her older sister's friend's cousin thought he knew, it was already Tuesday afternoon. Winston rode his bike over to Frenchie's building a few blocks away, the coat flapping dramatically in the wind, and then, together, they rode to the building that was, hopefully, where Brian Dolph lived.

It was on the far side of school, and Frenchie had to be home for dinner, so they didn't have a lot of time to waste. They sat across the street at first. That had been Winston's idea.

"If the teachers are tailing him, maybe we'll be able to spot them," he'd said as they locked up their bikes on a street sign. "We watch for a little while, then we ring the bell." Frenchie thought it was brilliant and told him so, which made him feel great.

So they sat on the stoop of the building across the street, side by side, in the usual order. Every now and then, a car drove by, but not a single one had a teacher behind the wheel. "They could be in disguise," Frenchie pointed out.

After that, Winston looked extra carefully.

"Bruno!" called a voice down the block, startling them. It was a man being pulled along by a giant mastiff. "Bruno," the man begged as he tripped over his own feet, "stop. Bruno, please stop. Heel. Bruno, slow down. Bruno, we talked about this."

"Bruno has his own plans," whispered Winston.

"Do not mess with Bruno," whispered Frenchie. Once they were past the stoop, she asked, "Do you think he could have been a teacher in disguise?"

Winston looked after him. "I've definitely never seen that guy in my life."

"I meant Bruno."

Winston slapped a hand over his mouth to keep from laughing. It seemed like you probably shouldn't laugh on a stakeout.

But Frenchie was merciless. "Maybe even two teachers, one as the front half and one as the back half."

She was the worst.

Also the best.

After Bruno, everything was quiet again. A cool, chocolatey wind blew, rattling the red and yellow leaves across the sidewalk.

"Cocoa punch!" Winston whispered, and lightly punched Frenchie in the shoulder.

She punched him back, harder. "What was that for?"

"It's a cocoa punch?"

She shook her head.

"You don't know what a cocoa punch is?" he asked incredulously.

"I have never ever heard of a cocoa punch," she said, laughing.

"I played it all the time when I was little. With—" Winston broke off. *With my dad.*

If Frenchie noticed that he was having a moment, she didn't let on. "How do you play?"

Winston closed his eyes and took a breath. "You know how sometimes you can smell the chocolate factory?"

She nodded.

"Whenever the wind blows just right and you can smell it, the first person to say 'cocoa punch' gets to hit the other person. It's a very excellent game."

"Uh-huh."

"You had the advantage, sitting west of me."

"I'm sorry, what?" She was laughing in a very anti-stakeout way. "Are you Marco Polo now? Sitting *west* of you?"

"Yeah." Winston double-checked. "You are definitely west."

"*How* do you know that?"

"I...just do. I always know which way the lake is," he said, shrugging. "I mean, not when I'm inside. But if I'm outside."

"Prove it." She smiled.

"Oh, I'll prove it," he said, standing up and fake-stretching. He cleared his throat as if he was about to start and then said, "You sure you're ready?"

"I'm ready," she said, laughing.

"That's northwest, the chocolate factory. Southwest, the airport. Southeast, Chinatown. Northeast, aquarium."

Before he could think of another place, she jumped in, saying, "Oh—are you going to Aquarium Night? We have to decide by next Monday."

Every fall, the aquarium held a special celebration night for all the eighth graders in the area. There were always rumors afterward about what did or didn't happen by the shark tanks and who totally fell in love with somebody from a different school and was going to be tragically gloomy and pining for the rest of the school year.

"I think Louise would kill me if I didn't go and see if there were any new exhibits," he answered. "She's obsessed with the aquarium. Or at least—"

"Wait—I think that's him!" Frenchie interrupted. *"Brian Dolph!"*

She was right. Brian Dolph was walking toward his front door, a gym bag slung over one shoulder. They snapped into detective mode. "Maybe the bag's full of money," Winston said as they watched him. "Or body parts."

"Except he's not the criminal," Frenchie said.

"Or so we *think*," Winston replied.

"Do you see anybody tailing him?" Frenchie asked.

They both stood, scouring the street in opposite directions. Nobody.

"Okay," she said. "Let's go."

She led the way, half jogging to get to Brian Dolph before he went inside. Thankfully, he dropped his keys and bought them a couple of seconds.

"Brian? Can we ask you some questions?" Frenchie said as they raced up the stoop. She got there first, leaning just a little bit against the door so that he couldn't unlock it. Winston stayed a step below.

Brain Dolph looked them over, frowning at first, and then, as they waited, recognition slowly crossing his face. "I know you. From Subito. Eighth graders?"

Winston nodded, more nervous than he'd expected to be.

"You're Volpe's kid. And you're Spot," he said, pointing to Frenchie's face, which reddened.

"Don't call her Spot," said Winston.

"It's fine," Frenchie muttered.

Winston knew she didn't really think it was fine. But they had official business to take care of, and it wasn't like they were going to convince Brian Dolph to be a nice person in the next five minutes. This was about getting answers.

"Brian," Frenchie began, "have you noticed anything suspicious lately?"

He snorted. "Like how suspiciously awesome I am?"

"No," said Frenchie firmly. "Like...*specifically*. For example, seeing a lot of your old teachers around?"

The question clearly surprised him. He drew a hand through his messy hair. "I...I don't think so....I haven't seen any of them since graduation."

"*Any* of them?" Winston asked.

Brian thought and then shook his head. "I'd have avoided them. They weren't too happy with me when I left. You know." He smushed his face to the side, sort of resembling the image stuck on the copier, and then winked at Frenchie.

Gross, thought Winston.

"Gross," said Frenchie.

"Hey, you guys came to me," he said, shrugging. "Everybody gets the full Brian Dolph Experience. My gift to the world."

"I think it might be overrated," said Frenchie.

But as Brian turned toward the door again, the reality that they'd gotten nothing from him made Winston reckless. He lunged for Brian's gym bag, taking it to the ground, and unzipping it as he did.

"Hey!" Brian yelled.

"Sorry, man," Winston said as he awkwardly got back up, handing Brain Dolph the gym bag, which now sagged open at one end. "I tripped."

"Whatever," Brian Dolph said, rolling his eyes as he stepped into the foyer of the building. They watched him through the glass as he went through the second door and vanished.

Winston sighed.

"Get anything?" Frenchie asked.

"A face full of super-sweaty gym clothes," Winston said sadly.

"Well, that does sound like the Brian Dolph Experience."

✦

They rode home, Winston's trench coat flapping, and no closer to an answer than before questioning Brian Dolph. Plus, there was something else bothering him now.

Outside Frenchie's building, with her mom waving from the second-floor window that dinner was ready and she should come inside, he realized he had to say something.

"Frenchie?" He glanced up, to make sure her mom wasn't in the window anymore. "I'm sorry about Brian. Being a jerk to you."

"Oh." She thought for a second. "I'm actually over it."

"I'm still sorry. . . ." His foot swung one pedal back and forth. "I'm sorry I didn't do more."

"Thanks . . ." Frenchie said slowly, "but I think some people, deep down, are just going to be humongous turds. It's not that it didn't bug me. But we've got a criminal ring to worry about. I can't care about Brain Dolph. And I'm not going to feel bad about myself because of him." She seemed almost surprised at her own words and then grinned at Winston. "When it comes down to it, I think you just have to let yourself be seen." She started rolling the bike toward her backyard, paused, and then added, "Except, obviously, when you're spying."

With that, she was gone.

Since there weren't family dinners at *his* house anymore, he rode around for a while, thinking to himself about Frenchie and about being seen and about the mystery. A trio of squirrels ran across his path, chasing each other in a line, their tails puffed out behind them, and suddenly, he knew what they had to do.

The idea kept him up all night, so that he was exhausted by the next morning—but he was so eager to see Frenchie that he got to school faster than usual, even lugging the Lonesome along. He found her in the usual spot, and as he dropped his tuba next to hers, they spoke over each other.

"What if we tail the tail to—" Winston said.

"We started in the wrong—" Frenchie said.

"You go," they said at the same time.

Winston covered his mouth and pointed at Frenchie.

"We should go back to what we know," Frenchie

said, talking quickly. "The teachers are at the center of it."

"Mr. Manning especially," Winston said, agreeing totally. "We go back to watching him."

"And I'm going to try to get another look at that accounting notebook. See if I missed anything."

They were probably the best detecting partners in all of detecting history.

In the minutes before the bell rang, they worked out a schedule for the day: At least one of them was dropping by the band room between every class. If they'd heard Mr. Manning correctly, that was when he'd be doing his criminal business.

The first bell rang, and they headed in to drop off their tubas. Already, something was happening. As they walked in, Mr. Manning was in the middle of the room, right in the empty trombone section, talking on his phone.

"No, no, no," he said, swiveling as he noticed the two eighth graders, and also banging his elbow on a music stand. He instantly doubled over. "Funny bone..." He wheezed from near the floor.

Winston and Frenchie slowly made their way over to the cabinet to stash their tubas, trying not to look like they were paying attention to him.

"I'm all right!" he said into the phone heroically. "Just...hang on..." Clutching his funny bone, he edged his way out of the trombone section and through the trumpet section, bumping the gong a little bit (which of course made it gong), all on his way to his small office, where he shot the two tubas a pained smile and shut the door behind him.

Frenchie immediately dropped to all fours and crawled over to listen at the door.

Winston stayed by the cabinets feeling useless, but certain that one kid in classic eavesdropping position was less suspicious than two kids in classic eavesdropping position. After an interminably long minute, she crawled back over and pulled him out into the hall. The two of them speed-walked to the language arts wing so they could beat the second bell.

"I couldn't hear much," she said, barely avoiding a collision with a tiny sixth grader. "But it was the good stuff. He said, *That's not what we talked about*, and a few seconds later, *We don't have that rigged yet*. So..." She smiled at Winston triumphantly. "They're rigging something."

Winston sat through class thinking of all the things that could be rigged. Elections. Tests. Those were important things. And hopefully, they could uncover more as the day went on.

There were six windows for criminal opportunity through the day. The order of spying was: Frenchie, Winston, Frenchie, both (lunch), Winston, Frenchie.

When Winston got to the band room before third period, he hadn't heard anything from Frenchie yet, so he didn't know what to expect. He stepped inside, past the seventh-grade orchestra members who were streaming out, and leaned against the wall. That was how they'd planned it. Then if Mr. Manning asked him what he was doing, he'd say meeting Frenchie. Mr. Manning would think they just couldn't get their timing right.

When actually, their timing was perfect.

Mr. Manning was at the podium, trying to worm out of a conversation with a concerned-looking violin player. At the back of the room, Winston saw two other teachers stick their heads out of the small office and wave Mr. Manning over impatiently. They were computer science teachers—Winston had one of them last year. They were nice enough.

Except that they were clearly also criminals, Winston thought bitterly.

It took Mr. Manning so long to get away from the kid that Winston had to duck out and run to history before he learned anything else.

He finally saw Frenchie again in fourth-period math, but she ran in as the bell rang, so they couldn't talk. Instead, he passed her a note:

2 COMPUTER SCIENCE TEACHERS.

She thought for a second, then wrote back:

Sardines.

Winston read it again. Had they come up with a detective code that he'd forgotten about? His note had been much clearer. What did she mean, *Sardines*? Or were the teachers rigging some sort of sardine delivery? That was a lot weirder than he imagined. He'd thought of a lot of options, but none of them were tiny, salty fish.

They finally got a chance to talk at lunch.

"No, not the *fish* sardines. The *game* sardines," she told him.

He still had no clue what she was talking about.

"It's backward hide-and-seek. One person hides,

everybody else seeks. When you find the person, you hide with them. Eventually, everybody's hiding together except for the last person who's seeking."

"They're playing sardines?" Winston asked.

"Not really, but something's driving them to Mr. Manning. When I went this morning, there was one other teacher there. When you went, you saw two. Before math? There were three. They may not be playing sardines, but whatever the problem is, it's getting worse and more of them are freaking out about it. And Mr. Manning? He's right at the center of it. He's the original sardine."

They spent the rest of lunch in a heavy silence, staring out at the cafeteria in front of them. Nice, considerate, bassoon-looking Mr. Manning, Winston thought. How had things gone so wrong for him?

There were no developments after lunch—each time they went by the band room, it was empty. And when they arrived for band, the Original Sardine looked considerably more shaken than he had that morning. His hair was ruffled, and his shirt partially untucked. He kept misplacing his baton during class, and when the last bell rang, he looked like a man who had run out of time.

Winston and Frenchie had planned to stay as long as they could, so first, before packing up, they had a very boring and totally useless conversation about the piece of music they had just played. It involved some pointing. Around them, their classmates packed up their instruments and headed home. Frenchie slowly got out a pencil to make a note for Winston on his sheet music.

In reality, they were feverishly detecting.

They observed as teacher after teacher filed into the room, each more worried than the next. Some of them talked quietly; some of them just took a seat, first filling up the flute section, then moving on to the clarinets.

They were going to have a meeting.

"Do we stay?" whispered Winston.

"It's risky," Frenchie said.

"But we might solve the whole thing," Winston said, biting his lip.

They nodded at each other. It was agreed. They were going to stay.

And thankfully, it was just chaotic enough that no one seemed to have noticed the tubas in the back row. Frenchie pretended to have a problem getting her mouthpiece out.

Winston was definitely going to sweat through this shirt. If there was anything he'd learned about detecting, it was that it involved sweat, all sorts of ways.

"Moss?" called out Ms. Brody, the dance teacher. "I have some concerns."

Mr. Manning (aka Moss) tapped his baton. The teachers, now filling all the woodwind sections, quieted down. Frenchie and Winston sank lower in their chairs, trying to disappear behind the music stands in front of them.

Mr. Manning spoke. "Listen, I know this is a change. But we can adjust. It just takes a little..." He held out his hands and made an abrupt twisting motion.

Winston gasped quietly. It looked very much like Mr. Manning was breaking an imaginary person's neck.

"I don't think *I* can adjust!" bellowed Mr. DuBard. Several other teachers rumbled in agreement.

"All right, all right. I hear your concerns," Mr. Manning said, his voice strained. "I'll do it by myself! I just need about a hundred and thirty pounds of—"

"No offense, Moss," Ms. Jardine interrupted.

Winston glanced at Frenchie, who shrugged. One hundred and thirty pounds of what?

Ms. Jardine continued. "But this would be a lot easier if Beth would just talk to Katherine."

"I *know.*" Mr. Manning sighed. "I agree. But Beth has Science Club, and she says that takes priority over everything."

Science Club.

Winston was so surprised, he dropped his mouthpiece and it clanged into the rest of his tuba. The teachers went silent. As one, they turned to look at the lingering tubas.

Frenchie waved.

Mr. Manning turned pink. "Er...helloooo there. Can you go ahead and pack up? We need to have a very serious teachers-only meeting somewhat urgently."

"Sorry," Frenchie said, getting up loudly, like she'd never had any intention of being sneaky or eavesdropping on the meeting. Winston thought she was probably a genius. "We were just going over some stuff. We'll go ahead and get out of your hair!" She casually walked over to the cabinets with her case.

Winston followed, and even though they took their time putting the tubas away, the teachers didn't say another word. Instead, the rows of teachers watched silently as the two eighth graders headed toward the door.

"Oh!" Mr. Manning said brightly. "You're not bringing your tubas home?"

"Not today," said Winston.

"Huh," said Mr. Manning.

"Huh," said all the other teachers.

They stayed casual until they were out in the hall, and then Winston and Frenchie flat-out ran for the main door, their backpacks slapping against them with each step. When they broke through to the sidewalk out front, the two of them finally stopped to catch their breath.

"That was weird, right?" Frenchie asked when she could talk again.

"The weirdest," Winston confirmed.

"I thought maybe they were onto us," Frenchie said. "Then they got weird. But teachers *can* be weird. On the other hand, we finally have a lead."

"And," said Winston, "I happen to know someone in Science Club."

CHAPTER 8

"YOU CAN'T JOIN Science Club," Louise said, waving a rolled-up piece of bologna at her brother. "It's mine."

Winston looked surprised. "But—"

"We have our own things. You have band. I have Science Club. And there are already way too many people in Science Club. It's overcrowded. So just don't." She layered the bologna on top of her mac and cheese.

"I don't want to join Science Club," Winston protested. He'd been doing his homework, and it was spread out all over the kitchen table.

"Good. Where's Mom?"

"At some kind of self-help-for-real-estate-agents meeting. She left a note." He pointed to the note that had slid all the way to the bottom of the fridge.

Their mom *still* hadn't noticed that there were no good refrigerator magnets anymore.

She didn't notice *any*thing.

"UGH," Louise said. She grabbed the note and magnet, and then pulled every other magnet off the fridge.

"What are you doing?" Winston asked.

"Fixing them," Louise said, and then, balancing the magnets, the note, and the bowl of mac and cheese and bologna, she started to leave the kitchen.

"Wait," Winston called after her.

She turned.

"I... um... still have some questions about Science Club?" He gave her a very hopeful, very toothy smile.

She eyed him suspiciously, but he seemed innocent enough. "Okay, fine. As long as you aren't trying to join." As she took huge bites of the bologna mac and cheese, she told him everything he wanted to know, and then, still chewing, dumped her bowl in the sink and headed off to her room. After changing into her pj's, she turned the lights off and stood in front of her small mirror.

The results were conclusive.

She was fading.

The glow was giving up.

She took a few deep breaths in the hopes of watching the glow surge as the extra oxygen filled her lungs and then traveled to all the cells of her body.

Nothing.

She did a few jumping jacks to get her heart beating faster.

No change. Without turning the lights back on, she flung herself into bed and buried her face into her pillow. It was fine. Experiments took patience. Scientists probably felt like this all the time.

She—very scientifically—punched her mattress a few times.

It helped a little, so she punched until her arms were worn out. Scientists, she thought when she finally stopped, must go through mattresses pretty quickly what with all the punching.

Later, she had messy dreams about a glowing bear, except he was doing all sorts of normal things, like brushing his teeth. The dreams tumbled on, one after another.

In the morning, she pulled on yesterday's clothes and felt a weird ache inside. Dreams were so dumb. They weren't made of real things like molecules, and it didn't make sense that they could affect a person this much. She shook it off and left for school.

It was a short walk, and she spent it stepping one foot on the sidewalk, one on the street, except for where there were cars in the way. Dr. O had mentioned once that it could be helpful for scientists to change their perspectives. That's what happened in the aquarium. Maybe she needed to change her perspective again.

By the time she got to school, she'd forgotten that the dream ever happened.

Every now and then, some other club met before school, but usually—like today—she was the only student around. She entered through the side door, passed a small group of teachers having a hushed conversation, and climbed the stairs up to the science wing. Dr. O's room was empty, which was no big surprise, but the lab was empty, too.

Of all the members of Science Club, Louise was

the most dedicated, but it still almost never happened that she was there alone, without Dr. O, even.

Not that she needed anyone.

Louise pulled her bight green box from the shelf and set everything up. Today, she needed to make a fresh batch of the G.L.O.P., but first she had to deal with those dumb magnets. She dumped them on the counter, the note fluttering out along with them.

Sorry I can't be there, it said. *XO.*

Louise folded the note carefully and put it back into her backpack.

She grabbed a strong magnet from the drawer of magnets and then spent the next few minutes trying not to think about the note and instead rubbing the weak magnets from home until they were charged up.

When she'd finished with them, she turned her attention to the G.L.O.P. She opened her notebook, but just before she started to measure out the compounds and mix them together, she glanced up. The room seemed unbearably quiet. Obviously, she didn't want the rest of Science Club there, talking endlessly about *everything*, but the empty silence gnawed at her.

She looked around. No one was there, no one would know. Louise made her way over to the computer by the wall, and after a few clicks, the first sounds of Kittentown Dynamo's title track "Good Kittizenship" hummed out into the lab.

Now things were really cooking.

As she measured and mixed, she sang along. The album really wasn't as bad as it seemed at first. Not that she'd ever, ever say that out loud.

The thirty minutes of jamming out and mixing compounds passed quickly, until a noise startled Louise. A noise sort of like a gasp.

She'd been right in the middle of singing the superhigh notes from the song "Step Off (My Tail)," but the gasp had been pretty loud, and she looked up to see Eleni standing in the doorway, holding her books and looking so happy she might actually cry.

"THIS IS NOT WHAT IT LOOKS LIKE," Louise said, panicking in slow motion. She was trying, *desperately* trying, to think what else it could be. She had really almost been hitting those high notes, though. That didn't happen by accident.

"It looks like you're having *fun*," Eleni whispered.

After a long, uncomfortable silence, Louise said, "That's weird. I definitely wasn't."

"Right." Eleni nodded slowly.

"And you were never here."

"I was never here," Eleni echoed, backing out of the room.

Once she was gone, Louise sighed. Deeply.

Eleni was going to spill those beans so fast they were all going to get bean whiplash.

By lunchtime, Louise had done a good job of avoiding contact with every other member of Science Club, so she was not thrilled when Eleni suddenly appeared by her elbow as she stood in line for hot food.

"Hey," Eleni whispered, startling her.

Louise tried not to look like she'd just jumped a foot in the air. "What are you doing?"

"Accidentally sneaking up on you, I guess," Eleni said.

"For the second time today," Louise muttered.

"I had a very valid reason for being there, but we can agree to disagree," she said, pushing up her glasses.

"Did you need something?" Louise asked, taking a few steps forward.

"Not exactly," Eleni said, catching up to her. "It's none of my business if you like Kittentown Dynamo or if you don't—"

"I don't," Louise jumped in.

"That's perfectly fine. I mean, *no it's not*, it's like exceptionally weird because she's the total greatest, but everybody has the right to their own opinions." Eleni kept talking while they inched down the lunch line, and Louise resisted the urge to somehow melt her. By the time the girl finally retreated and Louise got her juice and sat down by herself to eat in peace and quiet, she was thinking that maybe it would be better if she skipped out on Science Club today.

Or maybe—

She'd never cut school before. But what if she just left *now*?

She could avoid Science Club ambushes completely. Let them get it out of their system.

If she walked out of the teacher entrance, nobody would notice.

She smiled into her bologna.

CHAPTER 9

HOURS BEFORE LOUISE snuck out of school for the first time, Winston had met Frenchie at their usual spot that morning, nearly bursting with the news.

"Tell me," she said, leaning in.

"I asked my sister." He glanced over his shoulder. "Dr. Omanid's first name is Beth. Beth isn't *in* Science Club. She *runs* Science Club!"

"Aha!" Frenchie said, her eyes bright. "Do you know what that means?"

"What does it mean?"

"*I* don't know—I was asking *you*."

"Oh."

They resumed their usual positions leaning

against the wall. After a minute, Winston asked, "Does it bother you that we have all these clues and none of them make any sense?"

Frenchie shook her head. "That's how all mysteries start."

"Mysteries are like pineapples," Winston mused. "From the outside, it's hard to imagine the inside."

"Well, I think pineapples are delicious," Frenchie said, smiling.

The bell rang, and they pushed off the wall and headed toward the steps into school.

Halfway up, Frenchie reached out and gripped Winston's arm. He followed her gaze to the top of the steps, where a small group of teachers stood.

Staring right at them.

The teachers looked *spooky*, somehow. He pasted on a smile and waved. The teachers turned away in one motion.

After they'd gotten inside, Winston muttered, "What was that?"

"I don't think I want to know," Frenchie whispered back.

As they made their way down the hall, the other teachers standing by their doors seemed to have the same spooky look. And not one of them looked at either of the two tuba players.

Winston could have sworn they were avoiding him.

He just had no idea why.

It was the pineapple, all over again.

CHAPTER 10

LOUISE DROPPED HER backpack in the empty house, grabbed her helmet, and left through the kitchen to grab her bike. She had made a terrific choice. This was a million times better than having to hear about how *thrilled* everybody was that now she liked Kittentown Dynamo.

Which.

Ugh.

She really did.

All the songs were just really catchy, was the thing.

Whatever.

At first, she thought she was riding aimlessly

around the neighborhood but then realized she wasn't aimless at all—she had pointed herself in the direction of the stadium. The idea of sneaking back in crumbled as soon as she rolled up, though. There were about fifteen people clustered over to the side of the building, near one of the loading docks. She had to go past the loading dock to get to the rocks, and she'd never be able to sneak when it was like this. She was just about to turn around when she noticed that one of them was holding up a sign and the sign had a picture of the bear on it.

Her bear.

Louise locked up her bike and walked over to get a closer look. The crowd was protesting, although not very enthusiastically, and now she saw more signs, some leaning against their owners' legs, some lying on the ground. UNBEARABLE read one. FREE THE BEAR said another.

SEND THE BEAR HOME.

Her heart chimed in agreement, and she stepped up to one of the protesters on the outside edge of the group, an older man wrapped in infinite layers of flannel shirts.

"Does everybody know about the bear?" Louise asked.

"Everybody who pays attention." The man looked down at her and smiled. "But that's fewer people than you'd think."

She nodded. "I'm still in the research phase myself."

"You're in the what?"

She waved the question off. People just didn't get scientists. "So what can you tell me?"

"About the bear?" He scratched his beard thoughtfully. "Well, they just brought her in fifteen minutes ago for tonight's game."

The bear wasn't there all the time! That was why Louise hadn't been able to find it. Wait.

Not *it*. *Her*.

The bear was a *girl*. Louise started to smile, but then, realizing that the man was looking at her curiously, she made her face go back to neutral. "This is how it usually happens? They bring her in before the game?"

"Every game day for the last two months. I'm Carlyle, by the way."

Louise shook the hand he offered, and he continued. "They've been bringing her earlier and earlier to try to avoid us, but we're too smart for them. We have a secret plan." He lowered his voice as he glanced around. "We started getting here earlier, too."

"That's your *secret* plan?"

Carlyle nodded.

Just then, some commotion near the front of the group got their attention.

"What's happening?" Louise asked, craning her neck to see past the people in front of her.

"It's the guy who owns her. He's coming back out," Carlyle explained. Then he began chanting along with the rest of the group, "Bears don't deserve bars! Bears don't deserve bars!"

Louise joined in the chanting and slipped through the crowd to get a better view as the guy drove past. The truck was huge, and across the side it read: *Mr. Elegant's Exotic Animals*.

"Elegant, my butt," Carlyle said, appearing at her side.

"*Carlyle*," scolded the woman next to him.

"Pardon my language," Carlyle mumbled. "Gwen, this is... I'm sorry, what was your name?"

"Louise."

"Nice to meet you," said Gwen. She was just as bundled up as Carlyle, and the brown knitted hat she wore had very bearlike ears. She handed Louise one of the brochures from the large stack she was carrying.

"Gwen started this," Carlyle said affectionately. "She's the heart of the group."

"I'm just organizing," Gwen said. "We're *all* the heart."

They were getting off topic with all the heart stuff, so Louise was glad when somebody yelled, "Coffee's here!" as a food truck appeared.

"Our fairy godmother," Carlyle said with a big grin.

"The driver of the truck?" Louise asked to be polite. She was still thinking about Mr. Elegant.

"Nah, but he's nice enough. It gets real cold out here after the first few hours, and ever since we started, somebody's been sending us free coffee. All the truck owner would tell us was that it was our fairy godmother." He lowered his voice. "I think it's Gwen, but she denies it. Would you like some? It's *very* good."

"No, thanks." Louise wrinkled her nose—the only time she'd had coffee, she'd felt like there were ants crawling around inside her—but she walked with him to get in line. She needed to know more. "So, now what happens?"

"Not a lot, unfortunately. Elegant parks that truck in the garage somewhere," the old man waved to the giant cement structure a little ways down from the stadium. "We've never seen how he gets back inside. There must be a way in through the underground."

There was. Louise remembered racing with her dad through the long, flicker-y tunnel. He always let her win. Always.

Maybe she could turn this into a win, too.

"It's just him?" she asked. "Mr. Elegant?"

Carlyle nodded. "It's a one-man operation. You know those Russian dolls, where there's a doll inside a doll inside a doll?"

Louise nodded slowly.

"It's like that, but with trucks. He has the big truck, and inside of that is a smaller truck with a cage on the back. He pulls the big rig up to the loading dock, then drives the cage out and inside the stadium. After the game, he drives the small truck back into the big truck and—poof—they're gone."

Poof, Louise thought. *They're gone.*

At that moment, a reporter's van pulled up in front of the doors, and a buzz of excitement went through the thirteen protesters (two had already given up since Louise arrived).

"Maybe today's our day," Carlyle said as Gwen hustled toward the van, balancing her coffee and the brochures. The hope in his voice was almost too much for Louise to handle.

"I have to go," she said abruptly. He seemed slightly disappointed, but Louise gave him a quick smile. "I'll come back."

She headed to her bike, glancing at the brochure as she went. It was for a wildlife refuge just outside the city. Acres and acres dedicated to housing wild animals that weren't quite wild anymore.

As she unlocked her bike, the gears in her head started turning. It was still only sixth period back at Subito—there was still plenty of time before Winston would be getting home from school. She could work out a plan before he started blasting his tuba through the house.

She pedaled into the wind, remembering that conversation at lunch.

Eleni had been unshakeoffable. "It's none of my business if you like Kittentown Dynamo or if you don't—"

"I don't," Louise had interrupted.

But Eleni forged ahead. “Except, just in case you *do* decide to like her, she’s playing in town in ten days and it’s going to be INCREDIBLE. See, there are these fan boards, and she sometimes writes on them disguised as regular people, and a lot of so-called regular people are dropping hints about how it’s going to be the coolest, most out-of-control show anybody’s ever seen, like you won’t even know where to look, and it’s sold out, but I bet if you wanted to go, you could get tickets.”

Louise frowned, trying to follow all of that. “Why . . . could I get tickets?”

“Because she’s playing the halftime show for the Chicago Horribles.”

At the time, Louise had just wanted Eleni to stop. She’d wanted a quiet lunch across from somebody she didn’t know and wouldn’t have to talk to, somebody who wouldn’t embarrass her at all by declaring how much she loved a pop star in front of the whole Science Club, including the incredibly serious and very scientific Dr. O.

But now the bear was back in the stadium.

And suddenly, Louise realized that she knew exactly how to get her out of there.

CHAPTER 11

BACK AT SCHOOL, teachers had been avoiding Winston all day. They gravitated to the far side of any room he was in. Nobody called on him in any class. "I don't understand," he told Frenchie when they passed in the hall.

"Big pineapple energy," Frenchie agreed.

"It doesn't bother you?" he asked.

She shrugged. "I think we're going to get to the inside of the pineapple eventually, and that's good enough for me."

But then, about twenty minutes into sixth period, somebody threw the tubas off the roof of the school.

The inside of the pineapple was rotten to the core.

Winston, like everybody else in classrooms facing the courtyard, heard the yelling and ran to the windows.

The first tuba off the roof was Frenchie's.

The Canary.

It was already halfway down by the time Winston had edged into a spot at the window, so it took him a moment to understand. It took him a second to realize that this was going to be personal.

In the very next second, there was a terrible, heart-exploding, history-stopping *CLANG*.

Tubas were designed to make sound.

Just not ever, ever, *ever* that sound.

There at the window, Winston stopped breathing while his tuba appeared at the top of the roof's facade and then went over and then fell for an impossibly long time. It crossed his mind that it fell exactly the way he would have fallen. He would have fallen like that, graceful in the air, if not actually on the ground.

It was halfway down now.

His tuba.

The Lonesome.

Even though he didn't own it, even though it technically belonged to the school, that tuba was his.

He had held that tuba against his chest. He had lugged it home afternoons to practice. He had considered—though he would never admit it out loud to another person—how playing the tuba was almost like kissing someone, maybe, if that person was metal and if kissing sometimes made your lip muscles sore. He didn't have any other data on kissing, but anyway it felt very personal, what he had with his tuba.

This was planetary-sized destruction.

Winston wondered if Frenchie was watching. He needed to get to her.

On that thought, the tuba hit the ground, irrevocably.

✦

Toward the end of the period, Winston was called to the vice principal's office. He walked alone through the quiet halls, his head cloudy with grief.

Halfway there, a steady *click-click-click* echoed behind him, and he turned to see Mr. Manning, leaning on crutches that were making the noise, heading in the opposite direction, toward the elevator. His leg was in a cast.

Winston stopped right where he was.

Mr. Manning. He had been responsible for this.

He'd been the one at the podium, the one in charge of whatever the teachers were doing. The one person who should have understood the most how Winston and Frenchie felt about their tubas. How could he have done this?

The elevator opened and the *click-click-click* faded away.

Winston didn't get a chance to tell Frenchie about having seen Mr. Manning, because as soon as he arrived in the office, he was sent directly into the vice principal's smaller, inner-chamber sort of office, where she was already waiting.

Inside, he sat down in the chair next to furious, silent Frenchie, sat next to her the way he always did, everywhere, and tried to remember the last thing he had played on his tuba. He hoped it was "The Imperial March."

He wished he could remember. Had he played it one last time at the end of class yesterday? All he could remember anymore was the teachers meeting.

He was unaware that the fingers of his left hand twitched subtly, reaching for ghost valves to play the song, until Frenchie reached out and held his hand still.

It was the first time in the last hour that he could breathe enough air to want to cry. Even so, he didn't. This wasn't the place. He could tell Frenchie felt the same way.

The vice principal stood behind his desk. He was talking to somebody on the phone. "No," he was saying, "your daughter is fine. She's fine. No students got hurt, no, just tubas. . . ."

Just tubas.

His mind leapt to the pile in the courtyard. Who was going to clean them up? Where would they go? What did you do with a tuba that couldn't play anymore? As the questions stacked up, it occurred to him that there was something missing, something he should be asking that he wasn't. What was it?

The person on the other end of the phone talked for a while, and the VP nodded along.

Winston hoped whoever cleaned up the tubas was someone who cared about them.

The call finally ended, and the VP turned his attention to Winston and Frenchie. "All right, Mr. Volpe, Ms. LeGume. This tuba business—"

The two students nodded.

"As you may have heard, someone destroyed them."

"The teachers," Winston whispered.

"Um—well, that's—no—" the VP stuttered. "Absolutely not. The teachers would not have done that. We think it was another student. Where did you hear that about the teachers?"

Winston opened his mouth, but Frenchie cut him off. "We can't tell you that. Why do you think it was a student?"

"*I* can't tell *you*." He looked uncomfortable. "Anyhow, that is not why we're here."

"It's why *we're* here."

"I'm sorry, Ms. LeGume, I am not going to divulge any information related to the investigation of what happened to your tubas. I understand that you're upset, but we are handling this, young lady. It's not your responsibility."

"I. Am. First. Chair. Tuba." She bit off the end of each word. "It is my *only* responsibility."

The VP suddenly shifted his focus to Winston. "And are you humming the Darth Vader song?"

He was.

"No," Winston said automatically, feeling his face flush.

The VP cleared his throat. "Let me be very clear. Neither of you will do anything about this. Do you understand what I'm saying?"

"Oh yes," said Winston quickly. He had no interest in going up against the teachers. He was going to take that warning, and he nudged Frenchie's shoe with his own.

"I understand," she muttered.

"Good," the VP said. "As I have been trying to explain. Since the tubas fell off the roof—"

"They didn't fall," Frenchie said quietly. "They were pushed."

Winston suddenly realized what was missing. He raised his hand. "What happened to the cases? Only the actual tubas fell—"

"Pushed," Frenchie murmured.

"—so the cases, they have to be somewhere."

"Oh." The VP frowned and looked down at some papers on his desk, moving them around. "Umm... apparently, they were still up on the roof."

Somehow, that seemed extra cruel.

To take them out of the cases before throwing them.

"Okay," the VP continued wearily. "As I was saying. As a result of that unfortunate incident—"

Frenchie growled.

"—as a result, I will need you both to choose a new seventh-period elective."

All the air left the room.

"What?" asked Winston.

"What?" asked Frenchie.

"Why did you think I brought you here?" The VP seemed surprised that they were surprised.

"As part of the investigation," said Frenchie. "Obviously."

"Next-of-kin notification," said Winston.

"Um...," the VP said. He looked longingly out the window.

Frenchie put her head in her hands.

Winston hated seeing her like this. He hated all of it. After a moment, he stood. "We won't switch electives."

Frenchie looked up at him, astonished, and then joined him. "We won't switch electives," she said.

The VP sank his head into his hands. "But we don't have any tubas left."

"That's not our fault," Winston said, although he wasn't completely sure about that. If they hadn't stayed for that meeting, maybe the tubas would still be here.

Frenchie backed him up, though. She nodded. "Buy more."

"How?" he asked, throwing his hands in the air. "How can I get that approved? The board won't even give us the money for a new copy machine."

The two of them looked at each other. *Brian Dolph.*

The VP was in on it.

"Look," the VP said, softening. "I really do get it. This was an awful thing that happened. I've sent out a message to the district office, asking for any extra tubas other bands may have. No luck so far, but we can always keep our fingers crossed. In the meantime, though, we're only two months into the school year, we can't have you sitting in a class you can't participate in. That's coming straight from the principal's office."

He stood up, indicating that the meeting was over. Winston and Frenchie stood, too. As the VP walked them to the door, he said it again, like he wanted to be extra clear. "You'll switch electives by the end of the week. You'll switch or you'll fail."

CHAPTER 12

LOUISE WAS HAVING trouble keeping all of her hundred billion neurons in line. She wasn't sure how noticeable it was from the outside, but on the inside, it felt like they were rioting.

Making her have *feelings*.

She had to concentrate all the time, just to stay focused.

It was because of Winston. His tuba had been destroyed and he was miserable and Louise didn't understand why he was acting like this was the worst thing that had ever happened to him. It wasn't. She'd *been* there for the worst thing that had ever happened to Winston.

Even if he hadn't.

He was here now, though he was here and he was all over the floor. He'd spent all of Saturday lying on the floor of the kitchen. Every time she wanted anything, she had to step over him, when really she wanted to bend down to his face and yell, *It was just a tuba!*

Still, she tried to be nice, like some sort of incredible sister that he didn't even deserve. She sat down next to his head and reminded him what their dad had always said: "Sometimes you eat the bear and sometimes the bear eats you."

He didn't say anything; he just put an arm over his face and kept being inconsolable.

She said it again, louder, in case he hadn't heard. *"Sometimes you eat the bear and sometimes the bear eats you."*

"Thank you, I got it," said Winston, muffled from under his arm. "I have definitely been eaten by the bear today."

She left in a huff.

It was driving Louise up the wall. At least their mom got it, sort of—when she got home late Saturday, Louise overheard her telling Winston that he couldn't lie on the floor all day.

So then Sunday, he *sat* in the kitchen, still not doing anything, just staring out of the window. Half of her wanted to kick him and half of her wanted to make him feel better and those two things were not exactly compatible. Plus, she knew which one was the *right* thing to do, and that was why she went against all her better judgment and agreed to the bake sale.

"I want to call a meeting," Tib said to Science Club the next day.

Louise groaned and ignored her.

The other four gathered at the center table, and then, after noticing that Louise wasn't budging, they silently picked up and moved to the table next to hers. She continued to ignore them.

"I'd like to call this meeting to order," Tib said.

"Order," the other three said in unison. Louise could hear Desirée typing the minutes, but she refused to look up.

"I have been thinking," Tib began, "about ways that we could earn a little extra money to buy some more supplies. But then, er...the thing with the tubas happened."

Suddenly, Louise was listening.

"And I thought that if something similar

happened to the lab"—Tib gestured around them—"it would really make me feel better if another group, like, say, *band*, did a fundraiser to help *us* out."

Louise frowned.

"So I'm proposing that we have a fundraiser using the rest of the Science Club dues, but we use the money we make to contribute toward new tubas."

"What?" asked Louise. She must've heard wrong.

"Well, used tubas," Tib clarified. "They're cheaper. And we'll need to make back the dues, too."

"What a good idea!" said Eleni. She sounded *very* surprised.

"I think *I'd* like to do it," said Vi. She also sounded *extremely* surprised.

Several email notifications binged around the room. "You've all just gotten an invitation to the Tuba Fundraiser folder," Desirée said. "That I *just* made."

"Wait," Louise said, holding up her hands.

They all watched her carefully.

"A tuba fundraiser?"

They nodded.

This was too efficient. They'd already discussed

this. They wouldn't pass up the chance to discuss anything. The club meeting was a setup.

Louise narrowed her eyes at them. *"Why?"*

"Because," said Eleni innocently. Too innocently.

"Because of me?"

"No...?" Vi said, looking to Tib for help.

"Maybe a very little bit," said Tib.

Desirée still hadn't looked up from her screen.

"You just seem..." Vi began.

"Not so Mad Scientist..." Tib explained. "You seem more..."

"*Sad* Scientist," finished Eleni.

"Well, I'm *not*," Louise said. Could they see her neurons freaking out?

"Okay," said Tib.

"We don't have to do it," said Vi.

Louise looked at each of them.

"But we'd *like* to do it," said Eleni. "If it's all right with you."

It didn't make any sense, but it was also the nicest thing anybody had ever done. "Okay," Louise said quietly. "Thanks."

They cheered.

"Have you already decided what kind of fundraiser?" Louise asked.

"We thought a bake sale would be fun!" said Tib.

"Oh," Louise said. "I don't know how to bake."

"No problem," Vi assured her. "We don't know anything about baking either. But baking is just chemistry that you can eat, so we'll be fine!"

Over the next couple of days, they all brought in recipes that looked good. Desirée ran the numbers to determine how much they needed to make a good profit. Tib filled out the forms to withdraw what was left of the Science Club dues.

"Are you *sure*?" Louise asked before they handed over the forms to Dr. O.

"We're sure," said Vi, smiling.

The recipes piled up, and after some heated discussion (their favorite kind, it seemed), Science Club decided to make the bake sale a cookie extravaganza. They slowly narrowed down the choices to eight different kinds, including a whole range of Kittentown Dynamo–themed sugar cookies. Louise was surprisingly touched when she looked over during math and saw Eleni sneakily reading about cookie decoration instead of doing her worksheet.

Eleni spotted her and smiled.

Louise smiled back.

These were weird times.

They decided that the best day of the week to hold a bake sale was Friday, so after school on Thursday, the members of Science Club gathered in the lab and started laying out all the supplies they'd bought with the club dues. The chemistry lab had ovens and Dr. O had given them permission to use everything for the bake sale, so the lab was rapidly transforming into a kitchen.

One entire lab table was covered with bags of flours. Another one was for sugars of all kinds. One had bags of nuts and dried fruit. One table had egg crates stacked high. One was just the pans and the utensils and bowls for mixing.

This was going to be a lot of work, Louise suddenly realized.

But also, it was exciting.

"Are we ready to start?" Louise asked.

"Almost," said Eleni from over by the computer. "I thought—erm—we could play some music?"

They all looked at Louise.

She held up a recipe as if she was studying it, and said, as casually as possible, "That would be okay."

Eleni hit play, and Kittentown Dynamo sang out.

They'd just finished splitting up the recipes when a noise at the door made them all turn.

It was the woman in the suit. She seemed momentarily surprised by the music, then gave it a thumbs-up and held a cell phone in Dr. O's direction. "There's a little bit of a problem—do you mind?"

Dr. O sighed deeply and took off her readers. "Science Club, since you're not using chemicals or the Bunsen burners, I'm going to step away and try to solve this—you're all right?"

They nodded, and she left the five seventh graders alone with their plans to put together the greatest bake sale in all of Subito history, capable of not just breaking even but paying for two secondhand tubas on top.

They probably *would* have been all right if only they'd been working with chemicals and the Bunsen burners.

Desirée had the spreadsheet of the items they were baking, and who was responsible for which step in the process. They'd planned all the different kinds of cookies, and they dutifully followed the recipes—Louise wasn't sure she'd ever seen Science Club so focused. While the first round of cookies was baking, Eleni practiced drawing Kittentown Dynamo's signature emblem, a kitten with an *I*

Voted sticker, the design that would be the fanciest of the sugar cookies.

It took all afternoon, but finally, the baking was done and the tables that had once been covered with supplies were covered with cookies. They'd listened to *Good Kittizenship* so many times that Louise officially knew the whole thing by heart. They should have felt triumphant.

Except something was wrong.

The girls looked uneasily at each other.

"They don't smell delicious," said Vi. "Aren't they supposed to smell delicious?"

Eleni poked one. "We left them in long enough, right?"

"Yeah—why?" asked Desirée. She'd timed it all down to the second.

"They look dry. And also squishy?"

The five members of Science Club stared at the cookies.

"Should we . . . taste them?" asked Tib.

"That's what happens next," said Desirée, doubt in her voice as she consulted the spreadsheet.

After a brief pause, Louise stood up. "I'll do it. It's for my brother." She picked the basic sugar cookie with Eleni's icing decoration across the top.

It started to both goop *and* crumble as she picked it up. That wasn't a good sign. She took a bite.

And promptly ran to the sink and spat until the weird taste was out of her mouth. Then she turned to the rest of the club. "I wouldn't say it was good."

"Is it edible?" asked Vi.

"I also wouldn't say that."

"Was it the icing?" Eleni asked quickly.

Louise shook her head. "The outside of the cookie is all dry and tastes like cardboard, and the inside isn't cooked at all."

"It can't be all of them," said Vi, bravely taking a bite of a cranberry cookie. She made a noise and ran to the sink.

"Maybe the chocolate chips are okay." Eleni tried the one closest to her and then ran to a trash can.

Tib picked a snickerdoodle and then joined Eleni at the trash can before tasting it. She immediately spat out the bite.

Desirée looked at the cookies in front of her and took a step back. "I think that's a pretty solid data set."

They stared at the table as the realization of what they'd done dawned over them. An entire bake sale of disgusting cookies. They'd failed as chemists. And they'd spent all the Science Club dues.

Louise's heart sank.

By the time Dr. O returned, they were cleaning up. *Good Kittizenship* had ended, and nobody turned it back on, so the lab was silent now, except for the sound of cookies landing in the trash.

"What... happened?" Dr. Omanid asked, stopping a few steps into the lab.

"They were defective," Vi said.

"The chemistry seemed right," Tib said.

"Something was off," said Desirée.

"They do look a little—" Dr. O broke off as she put her readers on and examined a pile in the nearest trash can. After a moment, she looked up. "Where did you bake these?"

The five members of Science Club pointed at the largest oven, the one they'd picked to make it go faster.

"Oh dear."

"What did we do?" asked Eleni.

"That's the drying oven, for sterilizing equipment. You've very thoroughly sterilized all these cookies."

The Science Club stared at the perfectly normal-looking oven.

"You needed the *convection* oven. *That* one." Dr. O pointed across the room to the other, smaller oven.

Dr. O was very apologetic, saying that she should have been there, and Science Club ended later than usual—the only signs of the failed experiment were the flour dusting everyone's shoes and the fifty pounds of disgusting but sterile cookies in the garbage.

That was all their money for supplies, for the whole year, in the trash.

When they finally finished cleaning, the members of Science Club left together, stepping outside into the chilly evening air in silence.

"Maybe we can—" Eleni started to say.

"No," Louise cut her off. "Thanks, though. For trying. I'm sorry we lost it all." She turned and walked away before the knot in her throat could turn into anything else.

She'd been kicking herself ever since she'd taken a bite of the sugar cookie. She never should have agreed to this. "It was nice of you to try to help my brother," she called over her shoulder.

She hunched against the cool air and picked up the pace. If there was no money left for Science Club, her experiments would have to stop. And she loved Winston, she loved him as much as she was mad at him, but she already had enough to take care of.

The bear.

Her dad.

She couldn't help everybody.

✦

She slept badly, and the next morning, left the house just after 4:00 a.m. Now that she knew her best—and maybe only—chance to jailbreak the bear was in exactly two days, she had to get prepared, fast. She brought a flashlight this time, since she'd almost stopped glowing, and as she pulled up, she noticed a poster that one of the protesters had left behind. It had fallen by the side of the walking path, probably as they were leaving yesterday, and it read BEARS ARE PEOPLE, TOO. Louise agreed with the feeling of the statement, even if technically it broke several important rules of biology, and so she scooped it up and wedged it into the back of her bike after locking up. She edged out onto the rocks and crept around to the secret room. This part was the most nerve-racking, because if it was locked now, the entire mission was busted.

The door handle turned.

She didn't believe in signs, but it would have been a good one if she did.

She let herself in, and this time the soundtrack didn't surprise her. Instead, weirdly, it made her feel like the bear knew she was coming. She zipped up her hoodie, stepped through the thumb into the rest of the building, and crept through halls toward the security office.

She got as close as she could without being seen, squeezing behind a door that was propped open a few feet away.

Through the big glass panels, she'd seen that there were two guards inside, joking around about something. Eventually, they stepped out of the office, each heading off to do rounds on a different wing of the building. One of them, the woman, was going to walk directly past Louise's hiding spot—if she turned her head at the wrong moment, she'd see Louise through the small rectangular window of the door, staring right back out at her.

Louise held her breath.

At the crucial moment, the woman glanced down

to switch on her radio. But Louise wasn't in the clear yet. If the guard forgot something or just wanted to yell back toward the other guard as he walked in the opposite direction—she'd see Louise standing there, pressed against the wall. It wasn't until she'd disappeared around a corner and stayed gone for a few minutes that Louise finally breathed again.

She sprinted around the door, into the office. It was bright in there—the windows that had been so helpful when she was spying now made her feel totally exposed. She had to work fast. It took her a few minutes to find what she wanted—keys. They were hanging on hooks in a metal cabinet that was, ironically, unlocked. She felt momentarily bad for the guards, but then thought of the bear and grabbed the largest set she could find. There weren't any labels, so she'd just have to hope they worked.

This was what had kept her up all night. She needed to make sure she could get in, even if they locked the door to the secret room.

Keys in hand, Louise took a couple steps toward the door and then stopped. No one could finish doing security guard rounds that fast—could they?

She thought not.

Might as well poke around a little longer.

A flickering caught her eye, and through the windows, she noticed a wall of screens in a room *within* the office, one that had the words *HEAD OF SECURITY* stenciled across it.

She opened the door and stepped inside. The screens were security camera feeds from all around the stadium. She watched, entranced for a moment, as she found and then followed the two guards on rounds as they walked, separately, from screen to screen. She didn't know where they were exactly, but if she could see them *there*, it meant they weren't in the office with her, and that was comforting.

But it also meant that she'd definitely been caught on camera.

She studied the screens more closely and realized that they primarily showed hallways. And nothing anywhere looked like the secret room, or even the hallways in that wing. Maybe they didn't consider anything there valuable. Whatever the reason, they'd overlooked her way in and out. She was still safe.

Perfect.

She was just about to leave when a folder on the corner of the desk caught her eye. It was a large brown folder labeled *Bear Protocol.*

She grabbed it and walked back out into the main

office as she crammed the envelope in her backpack. Her fingers brushed something cold in there, and she made a quick decision. They knew she'd been there before. She needed them to think they just had a vandalism problem, and if she distracted them, maybe they wouldn't notice the missing keys and folder.

Plus, it was consistent.

Louise liked consistency.

She pulled out the spray paint and left a giant *V* across the room.

V for *Volpe.*

A noise in the hallway sent her diving behind a desk, her heart racing.

"What the—" exclaimed the guard.

For a few seconds, she thought he was going to stand in the doorway all night, which would be really inconvenient for her. But then he moved again, toward the part of the office that had a small sink and coffeepot. She heard him pour a cup, muttering something to himself, and then say, "I know you aren't done yet. . . ."

She froze. Had he seen her?

But then he continued. "The, um . . ." He sighed. "The ghost was here?"

There was a staticky noise, and she realized he was calling the other guard on a walkie-talkie.

The ghost?

Was she supposed to be the ghost?

Well. That worked for her.

She didn't stick around to hear more, though. Staying low, she crept toward the door and slipped out into the hall that would take her back to the secret room. As she ran, she smiled at the thought of the V she'd left.

V for *Volpe.*

V for *Very Soon I Am Going to Set That Bear Free.*

Once she'd made it to the bear paw, she took a victory lap around the room, ran into one of the Hibernators, and jumped on the bed, punching the air and whooping until she flopped down, exhausted.

CHAPTER 13

TYBALT RAWLS, HEAD of security, had just started to relax. Two weeks had passed since the helmet debacle, and there'd been no sign of Lenny Volpe's ghost. Maybe it was an isolated event, one of those things that you can't explain, and pretty soon, you begin to wonder if it even happened at all.

But then he walked into work Friday morning to find one of the night guards waiting outside the office. She was chewing a fingernail anxiously. Rawls immediately wished he could turn around get back in bed and start all over.

"Before you go in there," she said, "we all just want you to know that we weren't slacking off. And we didn't fall asleep or anything like that. It happened in the middle of a regular patrol shift, and we feel really bad about it, but we didn't see anything."

The head of security was no longer relaxed.

The woman stood aside and let him enter the place that should have been the most fortified of the entire stadium. Any other day, the security office definitely would have been voted least likely to be vandalized.

But *this* morning, there was a giant silver *V* spray-painted across the room. It ran over the desks of the other guards, over their stacks of paperwork, and ended in a point at the inner door of his own, private office.

The ghost was telling him something.

"We didn't move anything, sir," the woman said.

"Good job," Rawls muttered. He called a meeting of all the daytime guards, and instructed them to scour the stadium for anything that seemed out of the ordinary. Any sign of the ghost. Of course, he didn't use the word *ghost*.

He'd sounded professional. "This takes priority. And let me know the moment you find anything."

He was on his second cup of coffee when the walkie-talkie chirped at him. It was one of the patrol, asking him to please meet her at the Ursa Major Rotunda.

The Ursa Major Rotunda wasn't for the general public. It was only for the absolute fanciest visitors to the Horribles Stadium. There hadn't been many of those lately, and so it had been off the guard rotation.

The room—a huge round room with an overwhelming bear theme—tended to make the head of security feel very human.

Especially the sound effects.

The architect had built a small compartment in which she had placed a soundtrack for the room, one that played nonstop, whether anyone was there to appreciate it or not. All day and all night, nature sounds emerged from built-in speakers placed around the room. Specifically, the nature sounds of a bear preparing to attack, on loop, for eternity.

Bears, the room said clearly, were dangerous.

It was, perhaps, a job too well done.

But that was not for the head of security to say. He arrived through the door of the thumb and stepped out into the paw, admiring the view of the lake. The outside entrance to the room was private and faced the water, accessible only by boat, but it turned out that not that many celebrities owned boats on Lake Michigan, so it had never been used.

The guard cleared her throat, and the head of security snapped out of it.

"Sir, it's Hibernator number four." She showed him to the room, and he stepped inside, stopping just over the threshold. The rooms were fashionably cozy and perpetually ready for the next fancy visitor who wanted some privacy and a nap. But this bed was unmade. The pillows sagged. It looked like it had been slept in.

Rawls had been having complicated feelings about ghosts over the last week, but one thing he was still quite sure about. IF ghosts existed, they sure as heck didn't *sleep*.

So there wasn't a ghost after all. This was a Goldilocks problem.

"Sir, Kittentown Dynamo will be here in two days. The room needs to be secure in case she uses it."

"Who?"

"Kittentown. Kittentown Dynamo? She's doing the halftime show. You know..." She did a few dance moves, but the demonstration did not clear anything up.

The head of security was trying to figure out what to say about the young security guard's dancing, when, thankfully, an idea hit him. He waved toward the slept-in bed. "Let's leave this. Exactly as it is."

On his way back to his office, he fought off a headache. Someone knew he had a soft spot for Lenny Volpe. Whoever was pretending to be a ghost wasn't haunting the Horribles. They were haunting *him*. And he was going to catch them.

CHAPTER 14

AS THE HEAD of security was shutting the door of Hibernator Suite 4, Louise was riding her bike through the dark morning, exhilarated. She was a jellyfish on wheels, racing through the streets to get home before anybody noticed.

She came to a speed bump and flew over it, suspended in midair for a second.

A train appeared on the tracks overhead, its windows lit, and she raced it.

She was the queen of the morning.

Louise had left the secret room confident that no one was looking for her, and as she catapulted herself over another speed bump, she replayed the moment where the guard had walked into the office, almost catching her.

The feeling of having gotten away with everything was glorious. She arrived at the house, put her bike away in the backyard, quietly opened the back door, slunk into the dark kitchen, and then turned to shut the door behind her.

"Lou?"

She spun around.

Her brother. He was in the kitchen. Just sitting in a chair, resting his chin on the table, with the lights off.

"Win," she said, standing very still.

Leeches had thirty-two brains. If *she* had thirty-two brains, she wouldn't have made a dumb mistake like that, letting Winston catch her. She bit her lip, thinking of a lie.

Except he didn't say anything about the fact that she was sneaking into the house before dawn.

She slowly moved toward the fridge, but he still wasn't saying anything. It wasn't an ambush. So she grabbed some sandwich meat, pulled the plastic seal off, and rolled up a slice, and headed for her bedroom. She should probably change her clothes.

"Did you set up a bake sale for new tubas?" Winston asked.

She stopped.

"One of the Science Club people said something about it in the hall yesterday."

Ugh. Of *course*. "We were. It got canceled. There was . . . a technical problem. I'm sorry it didn't work."

"Thanks anyway."

"It's no big deal," she said gruffly. Then, suddenly, she remembered something. "Win—what if—"

"What?"

It was a bad idea. It would complicate things. She should forget about this and go read the Bear Protocol.

Except that her mind kept returning to the stadium. The huge room, where she found the spray paint. She knew what she'd seen in one corner.

A pile of drums, a solid inch of dust on them.

Nobody was using those drums.

And where there were abandoned drums, there were probably abandoned tubas.

"Nothing," she said.

It was just . . .

He looked so sad.

She sighed. "What if I knew where there were possibly some tubas? Tubas you could have."

He looked up.

"Tubas nobody would miss."

✦

Louise left Winston sitting in the kitchen, changed her clothes, and then headed off for early morning Science Club. It had been one whole day without lab, and she missed it. She was still buzzing from the trip to the stadium, and as she took the teacher's entrance and climbed up the stairs, she thought to herself that maybe this was the day she'd have a breakthrough on the G.L.O.P.

But then she walked into the lab and her brain snapped into focus.

Her notebook was already out on the table.

It wasn't the only thing; there were a few random items scattered across each of the tables, and Dr. O was putting them away.

"What's going on?" Louise asked, hearing the edge in her voice.

Dr. O turned. "Oh, good! After Science Club yesterday, some other teachers needed to hot-glue a few... things late yesterday, and they made a real mess searching for glue sticks and left everything out. *So* irritating. But, Louise, I opened your notebook to see whose it was so I could put it away—"

Louise still hadn't moved away from the doorway.

"—and you're doing some very interesting work. There's a real market for it."

"There... is?"

Dr. O nodded, swung by her table, and picked up the notebook. She brought it close and flipped it open, pulling over a stool.

Louise joined her.

"All of this..." She pointed to the notes about the chemical compounds, page after page of them, detailing all of her progress with G.L.O.P. "It's clear that you're perfecting your recipe and detailing the evolution of the mix, which is what all the big houses want."

That didn't sound right. "The big houses?"

"The big makeup houses. The special effects people." Dr. O looked over her readers again. "That's what you're doing, right? Making glow-in-the-dark body paint?"

Louise's stomach twisted. "That's... that's not what I'm doing," she said quietly.

"Oh? What did I miss?" Dr. O looked closer at the notes.

"I'm..." Maybe she could tell Dr. O *some* of the truth. "I'm trying to affect cellular respiration. And the glowing, that's just how I know it's working."

"Hmmm..." The teacher frowned and gestured to the notebook. "Do you mind?"

It's sort of too late now, Louise thought. "Go ahead."

Dr. O flipped to the beginning and read the notebook thoroughly, so focused Louise almost thought she'd forgotten about her. When Dr. O got to the end of the notes, she closed the notebook and sighed. She took off her readers and swiveled her own stool to face Louise's.

"I can see, more or less, what you were trying to do, Louise. And it's a good try. But scientists have to ask the hard questions. And I think the hard question that you have to ask is, could this ever work?"

Louise felt a pricking in her throat. "I thought so," she managed. "It was supposed to."

"The problem is that cells don't breathe like that. They can't absorb oxygen that way, externally."

It was like being in an earthquake, she imagined. Everything falling down, and no steady ground to stand on.

"You did good work," Dr. O continued, even

though Louise wanted her to stop. "But it's one of the hard things about science. Sometimes there are just factors you don't take into consideration."

Louise picked up her notebook.

"I think I'm going to take a Science Club break," she said.

Dr. O nodded, like she understood. "Just don't let it be forever. You are the founding member, after all."

Louise started for the door, but then changed her mind, instead going over to her green box. She pulled out the latest batch of G.L.O.P.

She shoved it in her bag.

And she left.

CHAPTER 15

WINSTON HAD STAYED at the kitchen table long after Louise went to her room that morning. He'd been too wired to go back to sleep, so he hummed "The Imperial March" and stared out of the window as the sun slowly rose.

There were tubas out there. He and Frenchie could have tubas again. They could be first and second chair again, and everything could be the way it always was, and for some reason, everything in his body was yelling no.

It was really nice of Louise. But he didn't want anything to do with it.

And he was going to have to tell Frenchie.

"She has real, actual tubas *that we can have*?" Frenchie asked in disbelief four hours later. They were heading toward the language arts hall, swerving now and then as they did their usual best to avoid all the teachers who weren't absolutely necessary. "Legitimate *tubas*?"

"I think so."

Frenchie looked suspicious. "What do we have to do to get them?"

Winston held up his hands. "I think you can just have a tuba. No strings attached."

She stopped short, and another kid bumped right into her. "What do you mean *I* can have a tuba?"

"I don't want one."

For a moment, he wasn't sure she'd heard him.

"I don't—"

"What do you mean you don't want one?" she interrupted.

They were in the way of the hallway flow now, but Frenchie didn't seem to care.

"It'll be fine," he said, starting to walk again so that she had to catch up with him. "You don't need a second chair to be first chair."

"I don't care about being first chair. I'm asking for *you. Winston.* What about 'The Imperial March'?"

He'd thought of that. Obviously. It wasn't like he *wanted* to never play "The Imperial March" again, but sometimes things changed, permanently, even when you didn't have anything to do with it, and there wasn't anything you could do to make it the way it had been before. Wishing that the teachers hadn't dropped the Lonesome off the roof would never make it true. It would never unclang that terrible clang. Some things couldn't be fixed, and there would never be another Lonesome.

He knew he was being dramatic.

But that didn't mean his feelings weren't real. They were so real he thought they might tear him apart, and he really didn't want that to happen again.

"Frenchie. I'm done playing tuba."

They'd arrived at their classrooms. Frenchie was quiet for a second as students pushed past them. Finally, she said, "You really don't want to play tuba anymore?"

"Frenchie." He took a steadying breath. "It's that I don't want to play *another* tuba."

She understood then; he saw it on her face.

The bell rang, and they darted in opposite directions, scrambling inside before they were officially late.

So there, he'd told her. That was definitely the worst part, and it was over, although now he was going to have to decide what elective he wanted to take. He sat through language arts, imagining himself as an artist or a drama kid. Or dance. He pictured himself doing a whole dance performance dressed as Darth Vader.

That might work.

So he was a little unprepared when, after class, Frenchie intercepted him in the hall and handed him note. He opened it up to see a drawing of a tuba, and then an acrostic.

To: Winston

U R Requested

Bridge on 18th Street

After school

He folded it back up. "I'm going to take dance—"

"Just come," Frenchie said quickly. "Please."

The imaginary dancing Vader faded away. "You aren't going to change my mind."

"Maybe I'm not trying to change your mind," she said over her shoulder, already on her way to her next class.

They didn't talk again after that, because Frenchie wasn't at lunch, and Winston sat in on the dance class, which meant there was no good time to back out. And he wasn't going to make her wait for him on the bridge all afternoon. So of course he went.

Frenchie'd gotten there first, and as Winston walked up, passing the bridge tower, where he imagined some old lighthouse keeper must've once lived, he saw her in the middle, leaning against a railing, staring out at the Chicago River. Behind her, cars flew over the metal grates of the bridge, making a steady clunk. At her feet were the two tuba cases and a grocery bag.

"As first-chair tuba," she said. "I decided we needed to throw a funeral."

For a moment, they watched the water, and then Winston closed his eyes. He could do this. It would help. He hoped. "Okay," he finally said, opening his eyes again and noticing how far he could see, how wide the sky was here. She really couldn't have picked a better place. "Let's throw a funeral."

Frenchie nodded, pulled out her phone, hit her Tuba Greats playlist, and then tucked it speaker-up at her waist so that the Rebirth Brass Band (the first on any respectable person's list of Tuba Greats) played in the background.

She cleared her throat. "We have all gathered here today—"

"All?" Winston raised an eyebrow.

Frenchie gestured to include the two empty tuba cases, one with a small yellow bird luggage tag still attached. "We have all gathered here today to say goodbye to the Canary and the Lonesome. They were more than our instruments. They were our friends. Our giant metal friends.

"We never expected to lose them so soon. We expected to graduate from eighth grade and to leave them behind, as we became ninth graders who played the high school tubas. Someday, Mr. Manning would have convinced some other sixth grader to play tuba, and the Lonesome and the Canary would move on. That would have been sad, sort of like breaking up with someone and then seeing them date somebody else."

At that, Winston nodded somberly. That would have been it exactly.

"But it was nothing compared to the awfulness of watching them get totally demolished in front of the whole school. No tubas could ever truly replace the Lonesome and the Canary. That is a fact. But as the great Janet Jackson says, 'We are a part of the rhythm nation,' and once you are part of the rhythm nation, you are a citizen forever."

Then Frenchie picked up the grocery bag and pulled out a handful of mostly red and yellow leaves that had definitely and very recently been in the street. She shot Winston a sheepish look. "I would've gotten flowers, but there was a time issue and also a money issue."

"They're . . . nice," Winston said, meaning it.

She smiled gratefully and then threw the leaves off the bridge. They both watched as the leaves swirled in the wind, taking a whole leaf lifetime to fall what must have been thirty or forty feet, eventually drifting onto the surface of the river below, where the current quickly swept them out of sight. Then Frenchie offered the bag to Winston, who grabbed a handful of leaves (a little bit damp even) and let them go, a few at a time.

"Do you want to say anything?" she asked him after his leaves, too, had vanished underneath them.

He nodded, but he couldn't think of the right words. Not far off, a train hooted sadly into the air, the notes blending perfectly with the Rebirth Brass Band still playing out of Frenchie's pants, and Winston wished he could translate the feeling of that sound into language. Finally, he said, "Goodbye, old friend."

The two of them fell into a sad, comfortable silence.

And then Frenchie reached down, grabbed her tuba case, and flung it off the bridge, yellow luggage tag flapping all the way down until the case made a satisfying plop into the river below, completely submerged, and then popped back up to float underneath the bridge and out of sight.

Winston gasped.

"I'm not sure why I did that," she said after a second.

"That is, like, the most littering at one time I have ever seen," Winston managed. He grabbed the Lonesome's case and clutched it to his body. "I'm not throwing mine in. Just so you know."

"*HEY!*" came a muffled yell, along with a series of banging noises.

They followed the sound to the upper window of the bridge tower. There was a very angry-looking man in there, yelling and pointing through the window. *"DO NOT THROW THAT IN THE RIVER!"*

The two of them looked at each other in shock.

"He's talking to you," Frenchie said.

Winston, still holding the case tight, yelled back, "Don't worry! I would never—" But he didn't finish, because the man stepped away from the window, and Frenchie grabbed Winston's arm and pulled him, running off the bridge the way they'd come.

"I think he's coming out," she yelled, "and I think we don't want to be there when he does!"

"Why did you do that?" Winston asked, trying to distract himself from how hard it was to run with the case.

"I don't know! I definitely already regret it," she panted. "And not just because of that guy. I was caught up in the moment, I don't know, burial at sea?"

"Burial at river," Winston said, wheezing.

And that made them laugh, which made the running even harder. They couldn't see the man behind them anywhere, and so they slowed down, not all the way to walking, but a sort of slow jog.

They were a few blocks from home when Winston noticed Frenchie looking at him hopefully. After all that, she was going to make him say it again.

"Frenchie—"

"Winston?"

"I'll help you get a new tuba," he said, wiping the sweat off his forehead. "But I'm going to stay in dance."

She nodded at him sadly.

That was going to have to be good enough.

CHAPTER 16

THE DAY FINALLY arrived.

Kittentown Dynamo was in town.

Which meant that Louise's window of opportunity to brazenly walk away with two tubas and a bear was also here. She'd prepared Winston by drawing a basic map of the stadium and explaining that they'd go in around the back, and while he and Frenchie were getting the tubas, she'd be taking care of the bear.

"What bear?" Winston should have said at that point.

"The bear that reminds me of Dad. The bear I'm going to jailbreak," she would've said.

"You are amazing," Winston might've responded.

"Thanks," she could've said.

But none of that happened, because Winston didn't seem to care enough to ask what she was doing with a bear.

"We'll just need one tuba" was what he'd said.

"You don't have to be weird about it," she'd said. "You can have as many as you want—it's a garbage dump. Nobody is ever going to be using those tubas again."

"One is fine."

"Suit yourself." Whatever. She'd keep the bear to herself, and anyway, he wouldn't have understood why she was doing it anyway.

Their mom was already gone when they got up Sunday morning, and according to the note firmly stuck to the top section of the fridge with the magnet that Louise had fixed, she'd be home late. By mid-afternoon, Louise was so impatient she kept going to the front door, opening it and looking out, before shutting it again.

"What are you looking for?" Winston asked from the living room, after the third time she'd done it.

"Nothing," she called back. It was true. She wasn't actually looking for anything, except maybe hoping the sun would get lower in the sky and they could finally get moving. Winston made three bologna sandwiches to bring along and added them to her backpack, which already held the Bear Protocol and the spray paint.

A little after 4:30 p.m., they hopped on their bikes and swung by Frenchie's. She was already out front, sitting on her bike, waiting for them, wearing the outfit they'd all agreed on: dark jeans, black T-shirts, and black hoodies.

Frenchie kicked off, and the three of them rode toward the stadium. Louise led the way, and none of them spoke until they got to the ramp over the train yard, at which point Winston grumbled loudly, "Are you kidding me?"

Louise just smiled and powered up it.

A few minutes later, they closed in, the stadium looming in front of them.

They rode past the protesters, and Louise waved at Carlyle and Gwen, who waved back. It was a relief to see them, even though she'd known they'd be there.

Her plan relied on them.

Once she was inside, she was going to find the cage in the loading dock, left unattended while Mr. Elegant parked his big rig. She'd drive it out to the protesters, and let them take the bear the rest of the way to the wildlife sanctuary. The excitement around Kittentown Dynamo would provide a perfect distraction, so by the time Mr. Elegant figured out what was happening, Gwen or Carlyle or whoever would be far away.

The bear would be safe.

A flutter of nerves ran through her. Just past the protesters were the Kittentown Dynamo fans, already gathering with posters and T-shirts. The Kittentown chaos was already beginning.

She led her brother and Frenchie past the fans and the protesters, over to a spot a few yards from the stadium, where they locked up their bikes against a sign post. From there, they blended into the late-afternoon walkers, some with dogs, some without, and followed the official path along the lake, until they turned slightly toward the rocks and began climbing across them, behind the stadium. The wind blew, making waves of the lake and smashing it into the rocks, so every now and then Louise felt the spray across her face or hands, like the lake was excited for her, for them.

She was humming something, but it took a few minutes for her to realize it was the title track of *Good Kittizenship*.

Vi had been right.

Kittentown Dynamo was changing her life.

They crawled to where the rocks ended and the dock began. After glancing in each direction, just to be safe, Louise opened the door and started to step inside. Behind her, Winston let out a squeak. She turned around to see that he'd backed up all the way to the edge of the dock.

"What's in there?" he asked, his eyes wide, hands in karate-chop position. Frenchie stood next to him, knees bent, like she might need to jump really high.

Louise hoped she never needed either of them in an emergency. *She* definitely hadn't been that jumpy when she first heard it. Not that she remembered, anyway. "It's just a recording," she said, trying not to sound impatient. Once they were all inside, she locked the door behind them and led them toward the thumb. She shushed them as she stepped through, and the three of them moved quickly down the hall. "Turning right," she murmured as they took the first turn.

"And here it is," she said, pushing open the door and flipping on the light. Huge fluorescent lights clanked on, one after another, deep into the cavernous room. "What'd I say? Garbage dump."

Next to her, Winston gasped.

She had to admit, it was awesome. The room was like a warehouse. It was obviously the place for people to dump all the weird stuff that didn't go anywhere else. The rolling cart that she'd borrowed and the spray paint were just the beginning. The room stretched away in front of them and also to the left—from the door alone, they could see the giant pile of drums, huge pieces of old parade floats, piles and piles of banners, and boxes and bins stacked on shelves all the way up to the ceiling.

A rolling ladder sat by the door.

"This is going to take forever," whispered Winston, peering in a box labeled POM-POMS: DISCONTINUED FOREVER.

"I think this is how those people who found the *Titanic* felt," whispered Frenchie, holding up a T-shirt cannon with a tag that said OVERSHOOTS: DO NOT FIRE.

"Hey? I'm going. Okay?" Louise tried to snap them out of it. "You get the tubas and then go back to the secret room. Wait for me there."

"Can we have our sandwiches?" Winston asked. "Just in case."

Louise handed over the sandwiches and left. She wasn't worried about her brother and Frenchie getting caught. Especially today, on a game day, the guards would stick closer to the center of the complex. The offices, the locker rooms, the field. Where the people were *supposed* to be.

She was planning to avoid all of that, too, by going directly to the loading dock.

To the bear.

She jingled the keys in the pocket of her hoodie.

She made her way down the hall, no hesitation in her step, until she was almost there. Then voices drifted toward her from up ahead, and she gave silent thanks for the curve of the hall. Without it, they'd have seen her already.

She veered off to the left, sprinting down the closest hallway, away from the voices, until she came to a door. The only other option was turning around, which didn't seem like an option at all, so she slipped through, and as the door closed behind her, fresh air washed over her.

Louise was standing in one of the four tunnels that led to the field.

Careful not to be seen, she walked toward the

mouth of the tunnel, scanned the field, making sure she was alone, and then nearly laughed when she realized what she'd done.

She walked out to the fifty-yard line.

The center of the galaxy, her dad used to say.

And the center of the galaxy was so still.

So crazy quiet.

Not at all like she remembered it.

It was like every fan and ref and cheerleader had been sucked up into the sky. As the thought crossed her mind, she glanced up.

A few clouds drifted over the stadium, but not a single person.

Bummeroo, her dad would have said.

Bummeroo, she would have said back.

But of course, he wasn't out here. Nobody was out here. She was completely alone.

Except for the bear.

At that exact moment, the bear was pacing inside the cage less than three feet away, just on the other side of the fifty-yard line, in the middle of the field. The last time Louise had been here, Winston stood in that spot. Now it was the bear.

And the bear was more bear than she had expected.

She was the realest thing Louise'd ever seen, not a friendly type of mascot at all, nope, she was an eat-you-up-because-that-is-the-food-chain-sucker kind of mascot. And the urge to let the bear out from behind those bars *right now* was making Louise sweat. She had been so ready for this, but all the plans she'd made suddenly vaporized. The wide-open space of the empty stadium was a vacuum, pressurized, pushing Louise closer and closer to the cage. The bear had Louise locked in her hypnotic, beady-eyed stare, and it was reeling her in, no doubt about it. A foot away from the cage now, and Louise was astonished by how sharp and dangerous and smelly the bear was.

She was going to rescue that bear.

She tried to open the driver's side door. It was locked. For some reason, she looked to the bear for help.

And then something shifted.

The wind. A cloud, maybe. The seven-million-year-old tectonic plates of survival inside Louise's blood cells.

The bear felt it, too.

Louise watched as the bear glanced away, like a punter checking the breeze, and then her head snapped back in Louise's direction. Those little black eyes bored right into her. The bear seemed to shrink into herself for half a second and then she opened up that dangerous mouth, leaned forward, and roared so hard, so hard, Louise felt her hair move a second before she did. And then she was running, tearing across the football field, like the bear was chasing her.

Why had she thought she could do this?

She ran harder, circling the cage, caught in the bear's gravitational pull, lapping the end zones and the sidelines while the sun pulled itself directly overhead, and the bear, stuck in the middle, watched Louise go and, from time to time, roared the universe.

What now, Louise thought as the air burned her lungs. *What do I do now.*

CHAPTER 17

GAME DAYS WERE always a little more exciting. That morning it was especially true, what with Kitten-town Dynamo's extra security arriving and wanting a walk-through to make sure that her giant cat head (Rawls was sure he'd heard them wrong) would fit in the hallways. So he was late to watching the feed from the new camera, the one he'd carefully placed in a dark corner of the Ursa Major Rotunda.

Now, with a cup of coffee, he was settling in.

For a while, it was the same as usual.

Then he leaned into the screen.

There was movement by the door, but he couldn't

quite tell what it was. And then, all of a sudden, he could.

He held his breath, leaning closer.

There was a kid.

Then there were three.

He checked the time stamp on the video. This had happened almost half an hour ago. He took another sip of coffee.

And then he ran, as fast as he could.

CHAPTER 18

EVER SINCE LOUISE had left them, Winston and Frenchie had been making nonstop Fascinating Discoveries. Like, for example, the box that said DEFECTIVE FIREWORKS, DISPOSE OF PROPERLY.

"I'm going to take a wild guess," said Frenchie, "and say that these were *not* disposed of properly."

"It's like we're football archaeologists," Winston declared from the top of the rolling ladder, finding approximately eighteen boxes full of footballs signed by former players.

Their voices echoed around them, but Louise had assured them that no one would be in there for any reason, and so Winston didn't let it bother him.

What did bother him, a little, if anybody'd asked him, was being back in the stadium.

"Flutes!" called out Frenchie. " Found some flutes!"

They'd started by looking around the drums, thinking the instruments might all be in the same area, but that turned out not to be true. There was no order at all. There was cheerleader stuff mixed in with football stuff mixed in with promotional stuff—the grossest thing so far was a box of cotton candy that had melted and fossilized over the years, complete with bugs frozen in it, like something out of *Jurassic Park*. After that, Winston looked a little more carefully before he stuck his hand into any of the boxes.

"Winston," Frenchie called from a few rows over. Her voice sounded weird, and not just from the echo. "You might want to see this. But also you might not."

Winston climbed down, slowly and steadily. He was totally fine at the top of the ladder, and at the bottom, obviously: It was the in-between area that was worrisome. But he landed safely on the ground and then walked over to the aisle, where he saw Frenchie five yards away, waving him over. He passed a cheerleader version of a clown car, and one entire section of T-shirts that read THE CHICAGO HORRIBLES, SUPER BOWL CHAMPS! Like everything else, they were covered in dust. There was no year on the shirts, which was smart—but even so, Winston had a feeling they might never get used.

He finally reached Frenchie, who looked unexpectedly serious.

"What is it?" he asked.

"It's . . . it's your dad . . . but, Winston—"

She was still talking, but he'd blown past her, his heart caught in his throat, and suddenly everything felt very, very up close, like those magnified images of amoebas you see, where you realize the world has so many more levels of close than you could ever possibly imagine and Winston reached out to touch his *dad.*

Except.

His hand hit cold plastic.

It was a mannequin.

Not his actual dad.

He couldn't believe he'd thought it might be his living, breathing dad for a second.

That was so embarrassing.

Of course it wasn't his actual dad. Obviously. Obviously.

"Are you okay?" Frenchie asked quietly.

No. Not at all was he okay. But he didn't trust himself to try to say so, so he just shook his head.

She came around him and put a hand on his arm, so carefully, so lightly, she almost wasn't even there.

Winston was so over people not being there.

And so he put his hand on hers.

It only lasted half a moment, and then something in him gave up, and he stepped into her, magnified-amoeba close, to let her hold him, and sank into her shoulder, buried his face against her neck, and let his rough breathing escape with her arms around him. And when he was calm again, they stayed like that for another couple of minutes.

Face to face.

They'd spent two years sitting side by side.

This was sort of new.

"I'm sorry," she said again. "I should have started with the mannequin part."

"It's okay," he said, stepping back. "I wouldn't have paid attention to that part anyway." He took one more deep breath and turned to look at the mannequin of his dad again. It wasn't the only one; there were dozens of them down that aisle, maybe even a whole team, some of them standing up like his dad, some of them missing parts. There were arms and legs and heads all around on the floor and the shelves. The mannequins wore the older uniforms, before the league changed the rules, before the uniforms became more like costumes.

Before his dad had gotten swallowed whole by his broken brain.

"What do you think they used them for?" Frenchie asked.

"Ads, maybe? Or maybe they were out front, so you could take your picture with the players?" Winston circled his dad's mannequin now. Something was different about him. The mannequin wasn't the right height, he thought, and then, like a punch in the gut, he realized that the mannequin was just right; *he* was the different one. He'd gotten taller since the last time he'd seen his dad. If his dad were here, for real here, this was exactly how it would be.

His knees felt wobbly, so he sat down at his fake dad's feet, and Frenchie sat next to him.

"Is this okay?" she asked. "I can go somewhere else if you want to be alone."

"It's okay," he said. It *was* okay. It was nice, even.

They sat among the random mannequin body parts for a while before Winston suddenly said, "I wasn't there when he left."

"Hm?" Frenchie turned to him.

"I was supposed to have been there, the day he left, but I wanted to go to the park. It was a nice day. Kind of a perfect day? And I wanted to go the park, and my mom was at work, and I asked him to take me. Which really meant that I'd take him. We'd walk there, and it would take a while, but I didn't care, I wanted to go and anyhow we were supposed to get him walking whenever we could. But he couldn't convince himself to go down the steps out of the house. He just stood at the top of the steps and shuffled his feet back and forth, and then finally gave up and went back inside without saying anything to me."

He hadn't meant to tell this story, but now it was coming, whether he wanted it to or not.

"And I just wanted to go, I didn't want to have to wait and help him down the stairs, which could have taken forever. So I grabbed my bike and rode. It was just as great as I'd imagined. I forgot all about him by the time I got there."

Frenchie let him keep talking.

"And then when I got back home, Louise was sitting on the front steps. She'd been crying. And Louise doesn't cry. She never cries.

"Apparently, she'd been doing her homework and suddenly smelled smoke. She ran into the kitchen, and she found him standing by the stove while these big flames shot up, burning the wall. He wasn't doing anything about it. So she yelled at him, I guess she yelled, *'GO! GO AWAY!'* to make him leave the kitchen while she grabbed the fire extinguisher and figured out how to use it. She was smart. She didn't want him to get burned.

"She didn't hear the door shut. She was too busy with the fire. She'd never used a fire extinguisher, but she's good at following instructions, so she read the label on it, and then put out the fire. When she finished, she couldn't find him anywhere."

"He did what she told him to do," Frenchie whispered.

Winston nodded. His head felt so heavy. He'd never told anyone the story. He never wanted to. "I should have been there. I shouldn't have left her to look after him." He dropped his head down into his arms. "She was only nine."

He felt her hand on his back.

"I guess he'd been talking about leaving and going to some rehab place. He'd been talking about it to our mom. About how he was only going to get worse, and he didn't want us to see it. My mom thinks that's what happened. That he would have left one day no matter what, but he forgot the part about going *some*where, somewhere specific. And instead he just went anywhere."

"I'm sorry," Frenchie said.

They sat in silence for a few minutes.

Then he shook his head. "We should probably look for the tubas again. We don't want to keep Louise waiting," he said, and then, surprising himself, he started laughing. "She is going to hate the mannequins so much."

"I wouldn't blame her. It's the weirdest," said Frenchie, nudging a stray fake arm near her foot. "But also, thanks. For telling me about him."

"Thanks for listening."

They got back to their feet and continued searching, although they didn't get as far apart as they'd been before. Winston wheeled the ladder over, and they became more methodical, confirming that each section was officially tuba-free together, before moving on. He was in the middle of pushing a smaller box out of the way, when, below him, Frenchie made a noise.

"I feel like there might be..." She stopped. "Winston."

Winston looked down and saw Frenchie's legs halfway sticking halfway out of the shelf beneath him.

"Winston," she called, excitement in her voice. "It's a tuba."

He hadn't expected to be this happy about it. He scrambled down the ladder, hitting the ground and crawling in next to her. She'd tunneled through some Halloween decorations and was pointing directly in front of her, toward an instrument case too big and bell-shaped to be anything else.

He looked at her and grinned. "Let's get it out, then."

They crawled out and began pulling all the Halloween stuff out. Even if the rest of the place was a disaster, and no one was ever going to want these giant spiders, Winston didn't want to contribute to the mess, so he stacked the spiders carefully to the side. When the way was clear, Frenchie crawled back in and pulled until the case slowly came out.

"It looks weird," Winston said.

"*Winston.* It's not a regular tuba. It's a *marching* tuba," Frenchie said reverently. "It's a *sousaphone.*"

And then, with all the care in the world, Frenchie unsnapped the clasps and pulled open the case.

She was right.

A sousaphone lay in front of them.

The sousaphone was made of concentric circles, and instead of being built to sit on a lap, it was *worn.* That was how people played sousaphones—tuba and human, moving like one.

They assembled it together, and Frenchie stepped into the middle, pulling it up and resting it on one shoulder. It wrapped around her like she was meant to have it there, and the bell rose up over her head, complete with a bear paw etched into the brass, and when she put in the mouthpiece and played a single note, it sang out of the instrument like the most beautiful whale fart the world had ever known.

They listened to it echo through the room.

"Oh, look," Frenchie said after a moment. She was pointing down at the shelf but looking straight at Winston. "There's another one."

Winston chewed on his lip. He'd meant it when he said he didn't want to play another tuba. But this wasn't a tuba. It was a sousaphone. Or maybe that was a dumb argument to cover up what was really happening, which was that he said goodbye to the Lonesome, and now he had room in his heart for another tuba-or-sousaphone. "This is what you were planning the whole time, wasn't it?"

"No, it wasn't what I planned." Then she shrugged. "But maybe it was what I hoped."

"Uh-huh," he said. And then after letting her wait, he smiled.

Frenchie helped him unearth the second sousaphone and shove all the Halloween stuff back in place. Then, with great solemnity, he opened the case. It was a beautiful instrument. Even with the giant bear paw on the bell. He didn't realize he'd been staring until Frenchie cleared her throat.

"We should go back to the secret room, probably," she said. "Louise might be waiting for us."

"I just need to do one thing first."

"Of course," she said.

And she waited, patiently, while he played "The Imperial March."

CHAPTER 19

WINSTON AND FRENCHIE headed back to the secret room, enjoying the new sensation of wearing sousaphones. They'd agreed that it would be impossible to get the sousaphones *in* their cases across the rocks—they were harder to manage than regular tuba cases—but if the two of them were *wearing* the instruments, they could use both hands for holding on and just move slowly.

"Besides," Frenchie said sheepishly, "I...er... probably don't deserve a case anymore?"

They were almost back to the secret room when they heard the distinct sound of someone running toward them. The hall was curved, so it was impossible to see who it was.

"Probably Louise," Winston said.

"It doesn't sound like Louise," said Frenchie.

Winston listened for a second and realized that Frenchie was very right, just as a man in a security guard's uniform jogged into view around the turn. He was definitely not enjoying running. He was definitely not happy to see them.

They stood very, very still.

"What are *you* doing back here?" the man barked, clearly exasperated. "This area is off-limits. You need to get back to the holding pen."

"Right," said Frenchie.

"Right," said Winston. "We're just... lost."

The man looked impatiently at the door to the secret room, and then told them to go back down the hall, take the second right and then the next left.

"Thank you," said Frenchie.

"Thank you so much," said Winston.

He watched them, hands on his hips, as they began to walk away, very slowly, and then, when he was apparently satisfied that they were headed in the right direction, they heard him burst into the secret room, yelling, "AHA!"

Winston felt himself go cold. "He got Louise."

"*Keep walking,*" Frenchie murmured as she dragged him forward.

"*But he got Louise,*" Winston said, looking over his shoulder.

"We can't help her if we get caught, too," Frenchie said.

"Then we should go back to the storage room," Winston said.

Frenchie shook her head. "We'd have to pass the secret room. It's too risky. We have to go forward."

Winston hated this, walking away from Louise when she needed him, but he knew that Frenchie was right. And that Louise would agree with her. She probably already had a plan to get away. *She's fine,* he told himself as they put more and more distance between them and the secret room. Lou was resourceful, way more resourceful than he was. If they got caught, she'd just be cranky when she ended up having to rescue them.

Frenchie led while he followed, and after a few minutes, he realized that she was following the guard's directions. They continued through the maze of hallways, which seemed to go on forever.

After a little while, they heard a voice up ahead and looked at each other.

"We're supposed to be here," whispered Frenchie.

"I am playing it very cool," Winston whispered back. "The coolest."

The voice got closer, and Winston tried to look totally sousaphone casual. A man talking into a phone appeared, barely glancing at them as he passed, and saying something about a uniform. "Fine, fine, if we have to get a uniform on it, I'll find one that fits. But I'll tell you this: I'm not the one dressing it."

When the guy's voice faded away behind them, they high-fived and kept walking. Winston's fingers danced across the sousaphone, playing "The Imperial March" silently, triumphantly. They were going to keep doing it, just like that.

A new noise sounded up ahead, and Winston and Frenchie pressed on, confident that they would be ignored again.

It was an odd noise, though, a sort of *click-click-click*, a sound that seemed familiar to Winston for some reason he couldn't quite put his finger on. He slowed, almost imperceptibly.

And still, the *click-click-click* came toward them.

His mind reached, trying to make the connection. It was so familiar. Something he'd heard recently.

The noise got closer and closer, and then, finally, the curve of the hall opened up, and Winston and Frenchie came face to face with a person dressed as a kitten.

The kitten wore a black leotard and ears with a little splotch of pink inside. His nose had a little black dot on the end, and whiskers were glued to the sides. Behind him, a tail seemed to swish.

The kitten was using crutches, because the kitten had a broken leg.

The kitten was Mr. Manning.

"WHAT THE—" Frenchie hollered.

"RUN!" yelled Winston.

CHAPTER 20

RUNNING WITH A sousaphone was a pretty inefficient way of running.

Even so, Winston and Frenchie were doing their best.

At least the hallway was wide and tall, which Winston was exceedingly grateful for, because otherwise, he and Frenchie would've been slamming the sousaphones into each other with every step. They backtracked until they came to another hall branching off to the left, and in a split-second decision, Winston took them that way. They were going to be so lost.

On the other hand, this would make it harder for Mr. Manning to find them.

"Why?" Frenchie gasped as they turned another random corner. *"Why is he here?"*

"Why is he dressed like a cat?" Winston said between breaths.

"Why are these sousaphones so heavy?" asked Frenchie gasping for air.

"*Yes*," Winston managed. He was almost shuffling instead of running now, because every step made the sousaphone crash down on his shoulder. *"Why. So. Heavy."*

"I...have...to...stop," Frenchie said, slumping against the wall.

Winston did the same, but he was careful to stay standing up. If he sat down, he was pretty sure he'd never want to get up again. So, in an awkward standing-up crumple, he tried to understand how Mr. Manning had found them.

"What does he want?" Winston asked, his eyes closed and his head against the wall. "How...could he know we were here?"

"Crime rings...," Frenchie replied weakly. "They have informants everywhere."

They heard a heavy door open, and the two

tubas frantically got to a more acceptable version of standing up—just as an enormous cat nose poked around the corner. There was grunting, and a luxurious voice admonished, "Careful on the corner this time," and then equally enormous cat *eyes* appeared.

The large cat glared into Winston's soul.

He stifled a scream.

And that was good, because the cat face was being carried by two ferociously muscular men who didn't look like they enjoyed being startled. They seemed *quite* serious, and as they walked directly between the two sousaphones, Winston realized the men were carrying an entire giant cat *head*, and lying across the top of the cat's nose and forehead was a woman wearing a gold-sequined dress that made her look exactly like a calico cat. Two additional muscle men followed, carrying the back end of the cat head, and behind *them* scurried a woman with a clipboard and a very worried look on her face. She looked familiar.

"Ow," said the woman at the top of the cat head, leaning down to talk to the men. "Can you please try not to bump me into the ceiling?"

"It's not their fault, Kitty," said the worried woman. "If we'd just taken the boat entrance, there would have been plenty of room."

"You know how I feel about water," the woman named Kitty huffed from above, sitting back against one of the cat's ears.

"Oh," said the clipboard woman, noticing Winston as she passed. She consulted her clipboard. "You're supposed to be in the holding pen, aren't you?"

"Er... yes," Winston said.

"On the way there now," said Frenchie, pointing in a random direction.

"Oh, wait," said Kitty. "Halt!" The men paused, not completely in sync, so the cat head shuddered to a stop and the woman had to hold on to the ear she'd been leaning against. "I don't remember asking for tubas—"

"Oh," said Winston.

"Um," said Frenchie.

"We can absolutely change it if you want," the clipboard woman said, flipping through the clipboard again. "We'll have to revisit the contract, though, and once the game starts—"

"I didn't ask for them, BUT I LOVE THEM!" Kitty cried. She pulled out her phone and handed it down to the clipboard woman. "Both of you tubas, come stand here so I can take some pictures."

Winston stepped toward the cat while Frenchie

tried to make her way around all the muscles, apologizing every time she made them jostle the cat head, and she kept getting the sousaphone caught on the whiskers.

When she finally got there, she had a scratch on one cheek and her hair was falling out of her ponytail, but that could also have happened when they were running, Winston thought. He felt an overwhelming surge of joy that if he had to be stuck taking a picture with a woman on a giant cat head, that he was stuck doing it with Frenchie. The flash went off.

"No," Kitty said. "Look at the camera, not at each other! Myra, turn off the flash!"

Myra, who mumbled something about having career regrets, took more pictures. Winston tried not to blush in any of them.

He suspected he was blushing in all of them.

When Kitty seemed comfortable with the number of pictures she'd gotten, she said goodbye, and the procession continued down the hallway, occasionally bumping into walls or the ceiling. One ceiling tile fell down as they went.

After the entourage had traveled out of sight, the two sousaphones turned to each other.

"What now? We go back to the secret room and wait for Louise?" Frenchie asked.

Winston nodded. "That guard has to be gone by now."

"Okay," agreed Frenchie. "Except I have no idea where we are anymore."

"I don't either," Winston said. "But I know how to find out."

Frenchie raised her eyebrows.

"It's on the lake side of the building."

"We need to get you outside!" she cried.

He pointed at the wall, where a small stencil guided them toward the field.

"We're following the arrow?" she asked.

"We're following the arrow."

It had been two years since the press conference and even longer since he'd come to the stadium with his dad, just to visit old friends, but Winston still had dreams of these halls, the kind of dreams you couldn't get out of, where you felt more and more trapped with every choice you made. He'd wondered, more than once, if that was how his dad felt when he was awake.

They took a soft right, into a section that was wider than the others.

"This one leads to the tunnel, which leads to the field," he said.

They walked on, together, until they reached the spot where the top of the tunnel turned to sky. Winston stopped there, with Frenchie next to him.

The stands were starting to bustle with activity, but down on the field, it was quiet. The players had probably already been out for warm-ups. The lines had already been refreshed. The field was so much bigger than he remembered, which maybe had to do with it being empty. Or almost empty. There was a cage out on the fifty-yard line.

A cage on wheels.

"Something's in there," Winston said, squinting. He walked toward it, curious, and then with a strange sense of dread as he saw the thing inside pacing in a familiar way.

"It's . . . a bear," Frenchie said quietly. "A real bear. How can they do that?"

"They do whatever they want to do," he said, his voice barely above a whisper. He felt so small out there. So useless. He hated this place. "Let's go." He turned toward the tunnel, but as he did, something on the turf caught his eye, something that looked exactly like a kid, sprawled out on the ground. It couldn't be. "Louise?" He started running. *"LOUISE!"*

All he could think was that the bear had gotten her. He didn't know why he thought that—it didn't make any sense. The bear was in a cage.

But he was terrified for her.

And then she sat up.

"Winston? What are you doing here? *I told you to stay in the secret room.* UGH." She rolled her eyes and then lay back down.

He wanted to hug her and also strangle her.

"Nice tubas, though," she said from lying down.

"Louise?" Frenchie asked as she joined them. "How did you get away from the guard?"

Louise sat up again. "What guard?"

"The security guard?" Winston said, but Louise shook her head. "When we were coming back to the secret room, this security guy ran in there and yelled. We thought he caught you. That's why we didn't wait for you there."

"It wasn't me in there." Louise seemed thoughtful. "But we should be careful."

"Are you done? Can we go?" Winston asked.

"These sousaphones are getting really heavy," Frenchie added.

"Take them off," Louise suggested.

Frenchie shook her head. "They're sort of... disguises, it turns out."

"Every time somebody sees us, they think we're supposed to be here," Winston said, grinning.

"It's like a magic trick," Frenchie agreed.

"Brilliant," Louise murmured.

Suddenly, another voice interrupted them. "Excuse me, kids?" An official-looking older woman in a Chicago Horribles windbreaker was simultaneously talking to them and gesturing to somebody down at one of the end zones. "We need to clear the field—where are you lot supposed to be?"

"In the holding pen," said Winston and Frenchie at the same time.

"Great," said the woman.

Wow, Louise mouthed to Winston.

"Let me just get you an escort," the woman said.

"No! We can find it," said Winston.

"We just came from there," said Frenchie.

"Uh-*huh*." The woman was already speaking into her walkie-talkie and waving over a considerably younger windbreakered person, who irritatingly talked the *entire* time he walked them from the field back into the stadium and down the halls and to a room with a plaque that read HOLDING PEN.

"Well, this is you," said the guy.

Nobody moved.

"Thanks," said Winston, who was absolutely not planning on going into the holding pen. "Guess you have to go, huh."

"Well, yeah," said the guy, who did not go.

"Too bad," said Frenchie.

"You're telling me!" the guy said, looking longingly at the door of the holding pen. "I'm so jealous."

"That we get to go in the holding pen?" Louise asked.

"You're not psyched?" he asked, surprised.

"I am not easily psyched," said Louise.

The guy shrugged, threw open the door, and ushered them in.

Louise, who was not easily psyched, promptly covered her face with her hands and screamed with joy.

CHAPTER 21

LOUISE THOUGHT SHE might hyperventilate.

"Oh, yay!" said Kittentown Dynamo. "It's those tubas! And a plus-one!"

Despite knowing that Kittentown Dynamo was going to be here, and in fact, *planning the entire thing around Kittentown Dynamo*, Louise had never imagined she would *actually be in the same room with Kittentown Dynamo*, and there was now a distinct possibility that she was probably going to die of awesomeness.

"Omigod," she said again for the millionth time in the last four seconds.

Then, finally, she realized how quiet the rest of the room was.

When they'd been pushed inside, the first person she noticed was Kittentown Dynamo, sitting in the middle, on the top of a huge cat's head, and that had been pretty much *all* she'd noticed, frankly, but now she took a step back and saw the other people, approximately fifty of them, all of them in black leotards and cat ears, every single last one of them a teacher at Subito School.

"Oooomiiiiigooood," she said one last, slow time, like a toy running out of batteries.

"Well, see ya," said the guy who had pushed them inside. Louise heard the door shut behind him. On either side of her, the sousaphones had gone still.

"You," whispered Winston.

"You found us." Mr. Manning looked back at them in horror. He stood at the front, but behind him, Louise saw almost all her teachers. Even the vice principal was there.

It was a weird thing to have to say about your vice principal, but there was no way around it. He had little whiskers drawn on his face, and he looked... *adorable.*

"You knew they were here?" Louise asked Winston.

"Are you here for revenge?" Mr. Manning asked, flinching.

"We are *so sorry*," said the VP at the same time.

"Remind me, what is he sorry for?" Louise asked out of the side of her mouth.

But before either Frenchie or her brother could answer, Mr. Manning blurted, "We didn't mean for it to happen, and we all felt just awful about it. But you understand why we couldn't tell anybody?"

"Oh, we understand," Frenchie said defiantly. "It's because of the crime ring."

"There's a crime ring that nobody told me about?" asked Louise. She shot Winston a look, not even trying to disguise her irritation.

"I didn't know either," Kittentown Dynamo called from the top of the cat's head. "If it makes you feel better."

It actually did.

"What?" Mr. Manning asked. "Which crime ring?"

"*Your* crime ring," Winston said firmly.

Louise was astonished. She'd never seen Winston like this before, standing up to a teacher. No, *all* the teachers.

"There..." Mr. Manning looked around to the

other teachers for backup. "There is no crime ring. We're an artist collective."

"That," Frenchie said, crossing her arms, "sounds like pretty much the same thing."

"Is it?" asked Winston.

"No," Mr. Manning said.

"So...you're not involved in illegal activities?" Frenchie asked.

The teachers shook their heads.

"But what about the money drop?" Winston demanded. "What about the tails?"

The teachers reached behind them and held up the tails currently attached to their leotards.

"Three hundred bucks *was* kind of cheap for legitimate surveillance," Frenchie whispered to Winston over Louise's head.

Louise couldn't stand it anymore. "WHAT IS GOING ON?"

"I'd like to know, too," said Kittentown Dynamo authoritatively. Then she winked at Louise, and Louise almost fell over.

"As the vice principal, I should probably answer that," the VP stepped forward, clearing his throat. "We've been preparing to be extras in Kittentown

Dynamo's halftime show for a few weeks. But... erm... it hasn't always gone smoothly."

Mr. Manning spoke, his voice heavy with guilt. "We're the ones who smashed the tubas."

Louise gasped.

"We knew that part actually," said Winston.

"You *did*?" Louise asked.

"*Do* we know that anymore? Do we know anything anymore?" Frenchie asked, indicating the kitten outfits.

"You were about half right. But you don't know how it really happened. The tubas—" The VP stopped and had to start again, like he needed the momentum to get through the sentence. "The tubas were already destroyed before they went off the roof."

Winston sucked in a breath. Louise hoped she wouldn't have to stop him and Frenchie from doing anything drastic.

"We were having that meeting about some new choreography," explained Mr. Manning.

"That was me!" Kittentown Dynamo jumped in. "I added it! For 'Always Land on My Feet.' I wasn't originally planning to play that one, but then it hit the charts and I had to, obviously."

"Obviously," Louise said.

"You two," Mr. Manning continued, talking to Winston and Frenchie. "You two were sitting in the meeting where we were talking about how one of us is supposed to be up a fake tree and then 'fall' out of it, but land on our feet—"

"The song is actually about how you pull yourself back together after a breakup, but it's a simile," Kittentown Dynamo explained.

"It's a metaphor," called out one of the language arts teachers.

"Exactly," Kittentown Dynamo agreed.

Several language arts teachers sighed loudly.

"The Chicago Horribles told us we could use their equipment today," the VP explained. "To lift Moss—Mr. Manning—up in the air, you know, because it turns out football teams have cranes. Which was very nice of them. But we needed to rehearse."

"And I am exactly the same weight as two tubas, plus their cases," explained Mr. Manning.

"Except it didn't go as planned," said the VP. "We were practicing in the auditorium, and we'd tied the tubas up to be counterweights. We attached them to the rigging by their handles. And we got

Mr. Manning up in the air. But we think the cases were sort of banging into each other, and as we tried to bring him down, the latches came unlatched, the tubas fell out and hit the stage—"

"I fell, too," Mr. Manning explained. "I did not, in the end, land on my feet. That's how I broke my leg. In the pursuit of art. But the show must go on, you know?"

"*YES,*" said Kittentown Dynamo enthusiastically. "*THE SHOW MUST*... Sorry. Go on."

"And so," the VP continued, "after the accident, we had no good explanation for how the tubas got damaged. We couldn't tell anyone about this." He gestured at his kitty-cat outfit.

"It's in the contract," confirmed Kittentown Dynamo. "I need my backup dancers to be anonymous. It enhances the mystique."

"So you threw the tubas off the roof," Winston said faintly.

"So we threw them off the roof," the VP confirmed.

"But we're so, so sorry," Mr. Manning said.

Winston and Frenchie shared a look, something unspoken passing between them, and then turned back to the teachers. Frenchie nodded slightly.

"You forgive us?" the VP said.

"Um, no," said Frenchie.

"I'd probably never forgive us if it were my bassoon," Mr. Manning muttered.

"We might, at some point," Frenchie said as Winston nodded along. "But for now, we accept your apology."

"Wait," Mr. Manning said suddenly. "If you didn't follow us here for revenge, what are you doing here?"

"We came for these," Winston said. "The sousaphones."

"I was helping them," Louise said quickly. She didn't need anyone wondering what she was doing there. "But I still don't get it. How does an entire school's worth of teachers get to be the backup dancers for the most important pop star of our time?"

"Remind me, who's the most important pop star of our time?" asked Winston out of the side of his mouth.

Louise turned on him. "How do you *not* know who Kittentown Dynamo is?"

"How do you *know* who she is?" Winston retorted.

"I listen to popular music now," said Louise.

"I listen to popular music, too," said Winston.

"TUBA SONGS ARE NOT POPULAR MUSIC." When all this was over, Louise was going to need to teach Winston some stuff about non-tuba music. For now, though, she focused on the teachers again. If teachers could be backup dancers for Kittentown Dynamo, then that opened up a lot of possibilities. Maybe a person could be a backup dancer and... a scientist, for example. "So? Can someone please for the love of Marie Curie tell me how this happened?"

"That was my doing," said a voice at the back of the room, and the teachers parted, revealing the one non-kitten in the whole room. She was sitting on a stool, typing on her computer. "I called in a favor from my niece."

"Dr. Omanid?"

"My aunt Beth!" beamed Kittentown Dynamo.

"Your aunt *WHAT WHO*?" said Louise.

"Hello, Louise," Dr. O said, looking over her readers.

"Hello, *WHAT*?" said Louise. She thought it was possible her brain might explode.

"I see you've met my niece, Katherine Omanid."

"She's the only one still allowed to call me that," Kittentown Dynamo said fondly. "When I decided to spell Omanid backwards, everybody else in the family liked it so much, they switched themselves."

"I prefer the original spelling," Dr. O said.

"So... that's basically how we wound up here," said the VP, shrugging. "Dr. Omanid was kind enough to give us an introduction because Kath—er, Kittentown needed a lot of extras for this performance."

"She's paying us," said Mr. Manning. "And we're definitely available for other events in the future, by the way."

"They're cheaper than professional dancers and much more enthusiastic," Kittentown Dynamo added.

"We really just need a new copier," the VP added.

"We can't handle this much Brian Dolph," one of the math teachers piped up.

"And a few days after the tuba... incident," Mr. Manning said, "we all realized we could use the extra money for new tubas. So, see, we were going to make it right again! We just couldn't tell anybody. It would have been a disaster if word got out."

"Why?" asked Frenchie.

"Mostly the secrecy clause in the contract. But also"—the VP grimaced—"this isn't an acceptable fundraiser activity." He whispered, "I really shouldn't be here. If the principal finds out..."

One of the librarians patted him on the back comfortingly.

This was a lot to process.

But Louise was good at processing stuff. As much as she would have loved to just keep staring at Kittentown Dynamo for the next five years, she had come here to do something, and she wasn't going to leave until she'd done it.

And now she had a new idea about how to get the bear out from under everybody's noses.

"We won't tell anybody you were here," Louise reassured the VP. "As long as you let us be in the show. We're already dressed." The all-black sneaking-around outfits that the three had on weren't that different from the all-black cat leotards the teachers wore.

"And you owe my brother," Louise added,

because guilt was always helpful. "You owe him *big*-time."

Mr. Manning chewed his lip.

The VP scratched behind his fake ears.

"Hooray!" said Kittentown Dynamo, deciding it for all of them.

CHAPTER

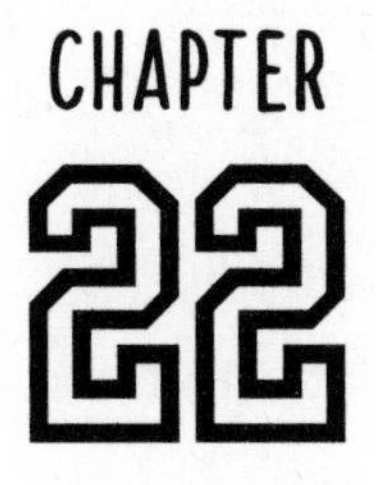

WINSTON SHRUGGED THE sousaphone off, turned to his sister, and, keeping his voice level, asked, "Could we please have a huddle to discuss certain topics that we are maybe not all agreed on?"

"Sure," said Louise innocently.

Winston did not buy it for a second.

Frenchie followed his lead, taking off the tuba and rubbing her shoulder as they stepped into a corner of the room, letting the teachers get back to whatever they'd been doing before.

"Why?" Winston whispered to Louise. "Why would you volunteer us to perform in front of a stadium full of people with *no practice*?"

"You don't need practice," Louise said. "You know how to play the tuba."

"Sousaphone."

"Whatever."

"No, *that is exactly my point,*" Winston said, trying to stay calm. "You can't just do *whatever* in front of fifty thousand people."

"You can also do some dancing," Louise said. "A little of each. Then you're spreading around what you can sort of do."

"You *did* want to dance," Frenchie offered.

"I was going to *take* dance," Winston said. He couldn't believe it. She was taking his sister's side. "I was planning to *take* dance, in which case I *might* have been good at dance, but that was all *in the future.*"

Louise looked like she had a lot of questions about Winston taking dance, but instead, she said, "You'll be a great dancer. Plus we have over an hour to learn. Plus *plus* we're quick learners."

"I really don't think I am," Winston said, glancing at the teachers as they hopped from one foot to the other, swinging their tails in one hand.

"This is the chance of a lifetime! I know an entire Science Club that would kill to be Kittentown

Dynamo's backup dancers," Louise said, glancing over at the pop star reclining on the cat head.

Winston bit his lip. Pop stars and dance routines and halftime shows—none of those were Louise things. She wasn't telling them everything. But he knew that the moment he said the wrong thing, she'd stop telling him *any*thing.

She'd slam the door. Again.

He hated how little she trusted him, and he didn't know how to change that.

"So?" she said, like she was daring him to come too close.

Maybe he could change it by trusting *her*.

"Okay," he said.

"Okay?" said Frenchie in surprise.

He nodded.

"Okay," Louise said. "Let's do this."

They turned back to the teachers, who were in pairs, silently mirroring each other.

"Oh, wow," whispered Frenchie.

"It's a warm-up," said Mr. Manning. He was a few feet away, doing the mirror exercise with the dance teacher, Ms. Brody. "Gets us in sync."

The three kids watched, until Louise broke the silence. "Can we have some of those cat ears?"

Several minutes later, Winston, Frenchie, and Louise had cat ears *and* tails, and were crowded around Mr. Manning and Ms. Brody, who had apparently collaborated on the choreography.

In one corner of the holding pen, there was a huge whiteboard that had football plays drawn on it. "I'm sure this isn't important," Mr. Manning said as he erased the whole thing. "All right, here's how it goes." And then he walked them through what would be a classic halftime medley of Kittentown Dynamo's greatest hits.

"BAD LUCK, BABY"

This was the first song, which, according to Louise and Mr. Manning, had been topping the charts for weeks. The story was about a down-on-her-luck black cat with some important revenge plans to take care of. Winston had trouble following the whole plot of the song, but it seemed like that didn't really matter.

"Kittentown Dynamo plays the main black cat, Kitty. The rest of us are like..." Mr. Manning thought. "Other, less important black cats."

Winston gave him a thumbs-up. "My name will be John Philip Kitten."

The other three looked at him.

"Even unimportant kittens should get names. I'm named after John Philip Sousa." He leaned toward Louise. "The first person to imagine a sousaphone."

Mr. Manning shrugged. "That's okay with me. Nobody else has names, but that shouldn't stop—"

"Brass Kitten," said Frenchie, raising her hand.

"I'll be iron, lithium, and neon," said Louise. Then *she* leaned over to Winston. "From the periodic table. FeLiNe."

"Okay," Mr. Manning said, sounding mystified. "Good work, all. Now, this is where we enter."

He drew a couple of lines, showing the entrance to the tunnel.

"Once we all get onto the field," he continued, "we spread out into three main kitten clusters." He drew three big circles to indicate the clusters and then, after a second, added ears to each one.

"Winston and Frenchie—"

Winston cleared his throat.

"Okay, I mean John Philip Kitten and Brass Kitten, why don't you join these two clusters." He drew two large Xs. "It'll be easier for you to grab your sousaphones later, since these clusters are closer to the stage. Um... you... science cat, you join this one at the far end."

The choreography for "Bad Luck, Baby" was all about walking in circles. Big circles, small circles, circles within circles. "It's all about making the audience feel like a black cat is always crossing their path," Mr. Manning explained. "Just try not to get dizzy."

"STEP OFF (MY TAIL)"

The second song involved lot of tail choreography. "As you might guess," said Mr. Manning.

After a few tries, during which Frenchie kept accidentally hitting Winston in the face with her tail and Louise kept accidentally pulling hers off, Mr. Manning suggested that they just stand still and swing their tails in a circle. "Everyone else is doing the choreography, so this will look... just fine."

"FERAL LOVE"

"The love in this song," Mr. Manning said, "is between a kitten and her giant ball of yarn."

Winston rubbed his forehead. Maybe he should be taking notes.

"Designated kittens will retrieve and bring to your clusters giant parachutes that have been painted to look like enormous balls of yarn from up in the stands. Er... I hope," he added under his breath.

"Mostly during this song, we will frolic."

"MEOW FOR NOW"

This was the ballad. It was the easiest, because all the focus was supposed to go to Kittentown Dynamo as she sang about saying goodbye to an old friend. It was sad and sort of mushy, and she wanted all eyes on her.

So for this one, they would all pretend to take cat naps across the field. "Curl up into a little ball, and just take a breather," Mr. Manning said. "You'll need it after so much frolicking."

"ALWAYS LAND ON MY FEET"

The song, about getting back up after life knocked you down, was the controversial recent addition. A fake tree would be rolled out onto the field, and Ms. Brody, the dance teacher, would climb up it for the first half of the song and fall out of it for the second half (with the help of the crane). Mr. Manning looked wistful as he described this part. "She will land, as I sadly did not, on her feet."

"GOOD KITTIZENSHIP"

The big finale. This was the real showstopper, according to Mr. Manning. It began with Kitty singing on top of the giant cat head in a spotlight, while a few lasers moved across the field behind her. The backup-dancing kittens would, obviously, chase the lasers. Then, as the song went along, and Kitty ran for mayor of Kittentown—

"Wait," Winston interrupted. "The band is also the name of the imaginary town?"

"*Yes*," said Louise. "There's a whole mythology."

"But—"

"*Quiet*, John Philip Kitten." She waved Mr. Manning on.

Kitty would win and become mayor. And during her inauguration, which was the last verse, the number of lasers would multiply and multiply and multiply until the whole field was patriotic lasers. "At that point, you should chase them in any way you want—that's the free-form part of the choreo—but just make sure you don't look up into the lasers," Mr. Manning said. "Whatever you do, don't do that."

"What—what happens if we look into the lasers?" asked Winston.

"Um... probably it burns out your retina. Sort of like looking at an eclipse." Mr. Manning was being much too cheerful about that possibility.

Winston put his face in his hands for a second. That was exactly the kind of thing he might do by accident. "Maybe I'll just close my eyes for the last song?"

"Actually, this is the song that Kittentown wants to have you play on sousaphone. While you were talking earlier, she wrote down these notes." He handed Frenchie a piece of paper with some music notes scribbled on it. Winston peered over her shoulder at it. On the bottom of the page was a little drawing of a cat with heart eyes.

"It's not hard," Mr. Manning assured them. "Just a little extra spice."

"Spice is the spice of life!" Kittentown Dynamo called out from up high.

"We don't know what she's talking about most of the time," Mr. Manning whispered, "but she's a musical genius, so who cares."

Since the finale was going to put the most pressure on Winston and Frenchie, especially with the whole not-blinding-themselves-by-looking-into-the-lasers issue, Mr. Manning suggested they go through the entire show once and then practice the last bit a couple of times.

Kittentown Dynamo agreed, so without further ado, they took it from the top.

The first song where they walked in circles was probably the hardest. Winston kept walking right when he was supposed to go left, and vice versa. Plus Mr. Manning kept calling out, "Prance! Prance!" and Winston wasn't sure that cats pranced—that seemed like more of a horse thing.

The tail spinning went okay, and the frolicking was exhausting—the teachers were doing all different kinds of dance styles, as far as Winston could tell. Some of them were sort of hopping; others were doing something that more closely resembled a line dance. Others were trying to breakdance. Mr. Manning was trying to use the crutches as part of his dancing.

The sousaphones got a chance to play their parts, though, and it made Winston feel a lot better, right up until the VP clapped his hands together. "Okay, folks!" he said. "It's time! Let's do this!"

There was a buzz as the teachers let Kittentown Dynamo go first, since she would be making a separate entrance, and then they started to file out, double-checking their ears and tails as they went. Winston couldn't believe how nervous he was. Frenchie stepped up next to him with a tiny clang as the sousaphones nipped at each other. She winked at him, and all of a sudden, he felt an awful lot better.

"Break a leg, everybody!" yelled Ms. Brody.

"Too soon," said Mr. Manning. "Too soon."

CHAPTER 23

THE BUZZER SOUNDED for the end of the first half, and the head of security scanned the crowd from his spot in the tunnel.

Rawls had people spread out around the stadium, but it was hard to see the details on that footage, and so all he knew was that he was looking for three kids. After spending most of the first half stomping around the hallways, he came out to get a quick breath of fresh air and check in on the game.

Not that he was expecting much. Sure enough, the team was being crushed by the Orcas, but the fans didn't seem to care—although on closer inspection, they were holding up big posters of cats, not bears.

Kittentown Dynamo fans, he realized.

Well. As long as *some*body was having a good time.

The players streamed off the field, passing him into the tunnel, heading for the locker room. The turnover on the field began, everyone quickly setting up for the halftime show, as Kittentown Dynamo's personal security fanned out and the tech crew pulled out the stage, and now the performers began coming out where the players had just gone in. The crowd screamed with delight.

He stepped aside to get out of the way. A grunting noise to his left made him jump, before he realized it was the bear.

It unnerved him to be around the bear.

It just.

It seemed wrong.

The bear was scratching its back on the bars of the cage. Probably trying to get the uniform off.

For some reason, they'd decided to dress the bear up in a uniform, which seemed redundant. The players were already dressed like bears. Why would a person need to dress the actual bear like a person dressed like a bear?

"Do you want to see it roar?" asked Mr. Elegant, startling him. The guy was sitting in a folding chair next to the cage, looking smug.

"No," the head of security said. "I'd rather not."

The man shrugged. "Suit yourself." He wore a T-shirt with a picture of the bear on it every day (*not* elegant, Rawls would have pointed out if there had been anybody to tell), and he liked to joke that he was the head of bear security, so it was sort of like they had the same job.

"Yeah," Rawls would say, trying to be professional. "Sort of." He needed this job, and he wasn't going to lose it by telling the guy to get lost. But boy, he wished that guy would get lost.

When possible, Rawls just avoided him. Which meant he rarely ever saw the bear up close. He wasn't far from the bars right now, and a few feet away, the bear sat, leaning against the bars, looking dolefully right back at him.

"Hey, pal," he said softly.

And then he noticed a presence by his elbow. He glanced down and saw someone else staring in at the bear. They were dressed like a black cat. Other black cats ran onto the field behind him, but this one was familiar. His mind worked slowly as he imagined the person without those cat ears.

And without that cat tail.

It was one of the kids. From the security footage. And she looked just like Lenny Volpe.

"See you soon," she murmured to the bear.

Then she ran onto the field.

"Bet you twenty bucks the bear could eat that kid," Mr. Elegant said.

Rawls just shook his head. What was wrong with that guy?

He looked out, finding the kid in the sea of cats again.

No, he'd bet on that kid any day of the week.

CHAPTER 24

AS THEY MOVED through the tunnel toward the field, Winston kept an eye on Louise. She didn't look up when the entire team ran past them. She didn't seem to hear Winston ask if she was nervous about remembering the dance moves. And then, when they stepped out of the tunnel, she made a detour.

He followed her, at a distance, as she jogged over to the bear cage and stood in front of it for a second. Then she turned, saw him watching her, and ran right past him to her place for the start of the show.

There was no way she really meant to do something about the bear. Right?

That would be dangerous.

But then the stadium was filled with the sound of cats meowing, and he had to hurry to get to his own starting place. The meowing echoed while Winston set the sousaphone down at the corner of the stage and then found his place, squatting with a bunch of the teachers in an approximate circle.

He watched as the giant cat head, which had been slowly making its way around the sidelines, finally reached the stage. The crowd cheered like a bunch of maniacs. Winston wondered if maybe he *had* been missing out on something. The meows were starting to become harmonic now, and then, as they began to crescendo, the cat head started to move.

The mouth opened wide, and Kittentown Dynamo balanced on the tongue, arms up, triumphant, a cat within a cat.

It was the bonkersest thing Winston had ever seen, for sure. A small human cat emerging out of the mouth of a truck-sized cat head should have been the only thing on his mind.

But he couldn't stop thinking about Louise and the bear.

So when the opening strains of "Bad Luck,

Baby" finally began, and the teachers began prancing in circles, Winston pranced with them, trying to figure out how to get across the field. Just when he'd edge over to the next cluster, the teachers around him pulled him back. "Thanks," he said over the music each time, like it was just a mistake.

"Meow," they replied.

But finding Lou, making sure she wasn't going to do something dangerous, was more important than anything else. He had to get to her.

Thanks to Kittentown Dynamo, he got his chance a few minutes later, when he discovered that the teachers were *very* into the frolicking portion of the evening. They didn't seem to notice as he frolicked right through them, all the way into the middle cluster, and almost into the far cluster. He'd nearly made it—but the song changed and a teacher snagged him by the sleeve, dragging him to the ground and yelling so he could hear, "Nap time!"

As he lay there, the turf prickling him, he worried.

He'd decided to trust Louise.

This wasn't trusting her.

But it reminded him too much of the days when his dad would cry for no reason or wear sunglasses inside the house for days and Winston and Louise knew something was wrong but nobody told them anything. It was rushing back, all of that, like Winston had crossed some invisible line, and he felt the way he did when he saw Lou on the ground earlier. He felt hot and panicky all over, and he needed to talk to her. It would be worth it, even if she stopped talking to him after this.

He *couldn't* trust her.

He had to know.

"Winston?!"

He rolled a little from his napping position, feeling the uneaten bologna sandwich smush in his back pocket. Frenchie was curled up a few feet away.

"What are you doing here?" she called.

"Just passing through," he called back.

"Everything okay?"

"Yes! Probably? I have no idea," he said, and then, as the lights swirled and the next song began, he got back up, slipping away from Frenchie and through the third cluster until, finally, he spotted his sister.

The smallest of all the cats.

And like before, she was staring at the bear.

He rolled, catlike, until he got to her. "Lou."

She hadn't heard him over the roar of music and the crowd singing along in the stands.

He tried again, louder. "*Lou.*"

She started, looking past him, at the rest of the cats. "You're not supposed to be here!"

"I'm just visiting!"

There was a brief break in the conversation as the music swelled dramatically, the tree slid out onto the field, and they all cat-stalked to their spots underneath its branches, watching Ms. Brody as she began her climb. Once they were in position, Winston scooted closer to his sister so they wouldn't have to yell so much. "Lou, why'd you come here today?"

"You know," she said, avoiding looking at him. "For the tubas."

"You said something about the bear. Before."

Louise let the challenge hang for a second as they watched Ms. Brody pass the halfway mark up the tree. Then she said, "I came because of Dad."

"Dad? What's Dad got to do with it?"

"Dad has to do with *everything*," she said, whipping around to face him. They were almost nose-to-nose now, and she was suddenly so angry he nearly fell off balance.

"With . . . with the bear?" he stammered.

"*With everything*, Win. Everything, every part of everything."

If he hadn't known better, he'd have thought she was about to cry. This whole time, he'd thought she was handling things better than he was. Maybe he was wrong. He asked as gently as he could, "Lou, what's happening with the bear?"

"I'm rescuing her," she said, so close to him now that the stadium dissolved around them. It was just the two of them, there at the center of it all. "And you're not going to stop me."

"That's *dangerous*, Lou. Dad wouldn't want—"

"You don't know what Dad wants!" she yelled and wiped her face on her arm, smudging her whiskers.

She was talking about Dad like he was going to come back, like he was going to walk into the house one day, just as randomly as he'd walked out, and Winston didn't know how to say it other than to just say it. "We already lost him, Lou. He's not coming back."

"He might!" she yelled again, like she could stop the last two years from happening, if she fought hard enough. "You don't know!"

"Even if he's out there, he won't remember who we are."

"But *I* remember who *he* is," she cried at the top

of her lungs, her voice breaking. “You act like he was nobody to us! You don’t talk about him, you don’t care what happened to him—”

The words sacked him, right there.

“Is that what you think?” he asked, while off in the distance, Kittentown sang a line about the ground being so, so far away.

“It’s what I *know*,” she said fiercely.

Somewhere above them, Ms. Brody was crawling out on the limb of a tree, and Winston didn’t know how to make his sister believe him, believe that he thought about their dad every single day. Missed him every single day.

And then he realized something else. She hadn’t been joking. “You’re really trying to find a cure?”

She bit her lip. “That is... temporarily on hold.”

“And now you’re really going to try to rescue the bear?”

She looked at him defiantly.

It was a terrible idea and whatever she was planning was definitely not okay, but all Winston could think was that he was proud of her.

Out of the corner of his eye, he saw as Ms. Brody fell in slow motion, somersaulting gracefully through the air until she landed on her feet, right on the fifty-yard line. The stadium exploded with cheers.

"Can we just talk about it?" Winston pleaded over the noise.

The final song of the medley began.

"Don't you need your tuba for this one?" Louise asked.

Winston glanced across the field and saw Frenchie by the edge of the stage, pulling on her sousaphone. He was going to have to run to make it in time. He glanced back at Louise. "Just... would you wait for me?"

She shrugged.

Great. He ran toward Frenchie. He'd play the song and then go talk Lou out of rescuing the bear.

It was one song.

She could hold on for one song.

CHAPTER 25

LOUISE HADN'T ORIGINALLY planned on stealing the bear in front of fifty thousand people. That was just the way it was working out.

As soon as Winston ran off, she scanned the field. The crowd was singing along. The first lasers had started up, and the teachers were chasing them. This was already chaotic, and it was about to get a million times *more* chaotic, if everything Mr. Manning described played out.

She made a quick decision, pulled off her ears, and ran over to where Mr. Elegant sat in his chair next to the cage.

As she crossed the field, she thought of sea

squirts, which were basically like sea potatoes, and they did this thing where they moved around as baby sea squirts but then, when they got older, they latched onto coral or something and never moved again. And when they did that, they ate their own brains, because who needs a brain if you're just going to sit on a piece of coral for the rest of your life and not do anything. They actually did that.

Mr. Elegant reminded her a lot of a sea squirt.

"Um, hi," she said, talking loudly over the sound of Kittentown Dynamo's mayoral campaign.

Mr. Elegant looked at her warily.

"One of the security guards was coming to find you, but then there was an emergency down the tunnel and she told me to give you the message?"

"What message?" he said, leaning back in the chair. "I'm enjoying the show."

"She said something about a fire in the garage?"

He sat up.

"Something about protesters getting in and starting a fire on your big rig? I don't know what she was talking about, but—"

He was already on his feet. He swore, looked around, and then took off in the general direction of the parking structure.

Leaving the bear unguarded.

Behind her, they reached the point in the song where Kitty won the election, and cheers went up around the stadium. The lasers were starting to get more intense, and the teachers ran around like frenzied, joyful kittens. She heard the first strains of the tubas as, somewhere, Winston and Frenchie were playing along on their sousaphones and Kittentown Dynamo was being held up in the air by her bodyguards (apparently, you could be a bodyguard-dancer) as she sang into the microphone.

It was exactly the moment Louise had hoped for.

She casually walked around the cage and reached for the driver's side door. *It opened.*

She'd been right. Mr. Elegant kept it locked when he was gone. But he didn't plan on *this* moment, and he'd been too distracted by the news of the fire to think about locking the door. She did a mental fist pump as she climbed up, pushing away empty soda cans, and shut herself in. Once the door clicked behind her, she allowed herself a smile. She'd gotten this far. The rest should be easy.

The Bear Protocol folder had contained a lot of useless information, but there was one game changer. There was a page with all sorts of details about the cage. Specifically, that it was electric. It shouldn't be too different from when she went to that kid's bumper-car-themed birthday back in fifth grade, when all the parents invited her places because they felt guilty. Those weird little bumper cars were electric, too. You just had to push the right buttons.

She pulled up her hood so the light would be less likely to catch her as she drove, slowly, deliberately, into the closest tunnel. From there, she'd go straight toward the exit, where she'd hand the bear over to the protesters. Her part was almost done.

She took a big breath and pushed the button.

She pushed *a* button, anyway.

A motor sounded at the back. But they definitely weren't moving.

Instead, there was a clanking sound behind her, and she spun around in the seat to see the bear, still dressed in a Chicago Horribles uniform, casually letting herself out and down from the cage.

Oh no.

Louise had opened the cage.

The bear stretched.

She shook out one leg and then another leg.

She flopped onto the turf and rolled back and forth. Then she sat up and looked around.

Oh no.

Oh no.

Oh no.

Louise had let a bear loose on the entire population of Subito School's teachers, who just happened to be dressed like small defenseless creatures.

And somewhere among them was her brother.

There was not enough *oh no* in the whole world for this.

And no one had noticed yet.

From her spot in the truck, Louise gripped the back of the seat so hard her knuckles turned white.

Okay. She'd let the bear out of the cage, so she was going to have to get the bear back in. In fourth grade, her class had done a whole unit about defending yourself against wild animals, which had seemed sort of unnecessary in the middle of Chicago until right now. She closed her eyes, remembering that, for bears, you weren't supposed to run. You were supposed to act bigger than the bear.

Louise steeled herself to be big.

She climbed over Mr. Elegant's stuff and out of the passenger side, quickly aware that the lasers had gotten stronger and brighter, turning the night fluorescent, and she had to squint to see anything, which was probably what was keeping the bear from going anywhere just yet. The song was building to the loudest, most celebratory moment, and it sounded like the entire stadium knew all the words by heart.

She took a step toward the bear.

And the bear took a step toward her.

Oh no. This was all going spectacularly wrong. Carlyle and Gwen were going to hear about this and they were going to shake their heads and make a sign that said DON'T FEED ELEVEN-YEAR-OLD GIRLS TO BEARS IT'S NOT GOOD FOR THE BEARS, and Science Club was going to study the stomach acid of large mammals, and her mom was going to be able to buy less bologna, and Winston was going to have to learn how to fix magnets himself, because the bear was taking another step toward her and she was going to get eaten. By the bear. Today, the bear was going to eat her.

She had meant well, at least.

She balled up her fists.

And then, somehow, over the crowd, she heard Winston yell, louder than Kittentown Dynamo, louder than the fans singing along, louder than her own heart, which was thundering inside her, heard him yell, "NOBODY GETS EATEN TODAY!" as if he knew exactly what she was thinking, because of course he did, and she watched as he charged the bear, who took a few steps back.

A boy with a sousaphone was, as it turned out, bigger than a bear.

And with the entire laser light show reflected in the sousaphone, the boy might as well have been the sun.

Bears, Louise remembered from way back in fourth grade, have excellent vision in the dark. Their eyes were perfectly built to see in low light. That gave them the ability to hunt in the night, to find the deer and rabbits that they wanted to eat. So maybe, when the sun, in the shape of a boy and a sousaphone, came bursting toward them, they would forget about eating altogether.

The bear retreated, and for a moment, Louise thought she might even go back into the cage, maybe everything would be solved by Winston and his sousaphone, and okay, she might not be able to sneak the bear out of here, but then again, Mr. Elegant hadn't returned yet, so maybe there was still time, and then, as the very last note of the song rang out, the lasers quadrupled in strength and there was a loud, electric *CRACK* and every single light went out in the stadium.

The lights had been so bright it felt like being plunged into the deepest, darkest night. There was a murmur around the stadium. Louise blinked furiously, trying to get her eyes to adjust.

She heard the bear grunt.

She heard her grunt again and begin shuffling, moving, and unless she was very mistaken, the bear was heading toward Winston.

It was really too bad bears had such good night vision.

She yanked off a shoe and threw it in the general direction of the bear.

"Ow," said Winston.

"Sorry," Louise said, feeling desperate as she threw the other shoe and heard it plop gently on the ground. Her eyes were finally adjusting, and the hulking shape of the bear was getting so close to Winston, and she had nothing left to throw but herself.

Human brains are fast. So lightning fast, in fact, that often they can solve a problem before the person even realizes there's a problem to solve.

Louise knew that, on average, a human brain

can process information at around 268 miles an hour. She was pretty sure that right now, her brain was working at two *thousand* miles an hour.

So without knowing how she was going to solve this problem, but trusting that her brain would figure it out, she ran. Directly at the bear.

And as she did, her heart, which had already been doing a very solid job, began working even harder, and all that extra air that she breathed into her lungs powered its way into her bloodstream, and there was, inside her, an electric *CRACK*, and suddenly there was light, and *it was Louise*, she was glowing, fiercer, stronger than she had ever glowed with G.L.O.P., and if Winston and his sousaphone had been the sun, now she was the moon, bright and cool and *enough*, and the bear turned, blinking at her, unsure, holding up a paw to shield her eyes, while Louise yelled, "WIN! GO!"

Winston turned on his heels and made a break for the closest tunnel.

She stopped a few feet away from the disoriented bear. After a few more dissatisfied grunts, the bear shook herself all over and then lifted her delicate little nose in the air and sniffed. And, with the attitude of somebody who has all the time in the world, the bear started strolling away from Louise and toward Winston.

Louise ran after both of them, and as she went, she heard the sound of the entire stadium coming to their feet and cheering behind her. They thought it was part of the show.

She wished.

CHAPTER 26

FIRST IT WAS usual sit sit sit.

But *then* feet on the grass YEAH GRASS and then boom the light, then whew lights out, then boom the light from smallest small human. Big day.

Ugh.

Just wanted snack. Followed snack off green green grass into long deep cave.

Snack ran.

So bear ran for snack.

Snackity Snack Snack Snack Snackity Snack Snackity Snack Snack Snack Snack Snackity Snack Snack Snack Snackity Snack Snack Snack Snackity

Snack Snack Snackity Snackity Snack Snack Snack Snackity Snack Snackity Snack Snack Snack Snack Snackity Snack Snack Snack Snackity Snack Snack Snack Snackity Snack Snack Snackity Snackity Snack Snack Snack Snackity Snack Snackity Snack Snack Snack Snack Snackity Snack Snack Snack Snackity Snack Snack Snack Snackity Snack Snack Snack Snackity Snackity Snackity Snack Snack Snack Snackity Snack Snackity Snack Snack Snack Snack Snack-ity Snack Snack Snack Snackity Snack Snack Snack Snackity Snack Snack Snackity Snackity Snack Snack Snack Snackity Snack Snackity Snack Snack Snack Snack Snackity Snack Snack Snack Snackity Snack Snack Snack Snackity Snack Snack Snackity

Slo down snack.

Snack Snack Snack Snackity Snack Snack Snack Snackity Snack Snack Snackity Snackity Snack Snack Snack Snackity Snack Snackity Snack Snack Snack Snack Snackity Snack Snack Snack Snackity Snack Snack Snack Snackity Snack Snack Snack Snackity Snackity

Cave went forever

and snack led bear on and on and on into final cave

right
into the sound
of
somebear's
mama.

CHAPTER 27

LOUISE STEPPED INTO the secret room, her weapon raised.

Her weapon was a plastic stand that pointed the way toward the bathrooms. She'd grabbed it during the pursuit, right when all the lights came back on, and hadn't been sure it would stop a rampaging bear, but it was better than nothing.

There was a pile of metal and fur in the middle of the room.

"Winston?" she whispered, panicky.

"I'm okay," Winston said from underneath the sousaphone. The bear was nestled against it, one paw thrown over the instrument. The other paw was holding a bologna sandwich that the bear was licking.

"It took my sandwich," Winston whispered. He was stuck looking straight up, but he didn't seem like he was in pain or anything.

"I can see that." Louise stayed close to the door.

"I'm pretending it's just Chewbacca."

Of course he was.

The bear sang along to the sound effects for a moment and then returned to the bologna sandwich.

"Can you get out of there?" she asked. "Without, you know, getting mauled."

"How about *Darth* Mauled."

"How about it would really be great *if you could focus*," Louise said firmly, genuinely concerned that her brother's fandom was going to get him eaten.

But the bear didn't seem concerned with anything and, after polishing off the sandwich, yawned and stretched out for a nap. After several long, tense seconds, Winston tried to wriggle out.

The bear shifted, and Louise hoisted the bathroom sign again, but Winston froze and the bear settled down. Carefully, Winston freed an arm, and then his head, and then, scooting slowly, his torso and other arm. At that point, he rolled over and crawled out, away. He ended up on the opposite side of the room from Louise, the sleeping bear between them. He could escape through the door to the outside if he needed to.

The bear murmured peacefully.

It didn't look like he needed to.

So everybody was safe, including the bear, but Louise wasn't sure what to do next. The plan to drive the bear to the protesters was out. And she couldn't bring the protesters *to the bear.* The bear didn't look like it was interested in going anywhere else.

On the other hand, she was so glad Winston was safe, she almost didn't even care.

"What happened to you?" he asked her. "How did you do that?"

"I just grabbed it from outside the bathroom," she said, putting the sign down gently so it wouldn't make a noise that might disturb the bear.

"Oh, not that. The part where you turned radioactive?"

Right. She'd forgotten. "It's my experiment. I think." She looked at her hands, which had gone back to normal. "Dr. O told me it was just superficial. Body paint."

"That was body paint?" Winston asked.

Louise shook her head in wonder and then looked up at Winston. "I didn't put it on. It's still in my bag. I don't know what I did, but I think I maybe changed my cellular respiration."

"Of course you did," Winston said, smiling.

"Win, I didn't mean it," she said urgently, before either of them could be eaten by a bear and then it could never be said. "I... I don't think you don't care about Dad. You just made me so mad."

"I know," Winston said, turning serious again. "I don't know what I did to make you feel like that, but I'm sorry."

"You... stopped talking about him," Louise said. "It was like he wasn't really gone as long as we talked about him, but you didn't even want to talk about him."

Winston didn't say anything.

"And what if they solve it, and we can't find him to tell him, and he misses out on the cure?" Louise asked quietly.

Winston thought for a second and then nodded. "It's why I liked playing 'The Imperial March,'"

"Darth Vader reminds you of Dad?"

He shrugged. "They both wore helmets."

Louise smiled.

"Kidding." Winston said. "It...it's because Darth Vader has a theme song."

"So?"

"And don't you wish Dad had a theme song? When you hear 'The Imperial March,' you know Darth Vader is right around the corner, even when he's not. You *feel* him. But then after the Lonesome—after my tuba got destroyed, I realized that maybe I was using the tuba to just fill up the space that Dad left, sort of? And that I can't just keep replacing him with tubas forever and ever. It's like, it's not fair to Dad. Or the tubas."

"Or you," Louise said quietly.

He didn't say anything for a second. "Yeah, maybe. I hadn't thought of that."

"You're welcome."

He rolled his eyes, exactly like she expected him to, and she grinned at him.

Then he shrugged and said, "So that's why I was going to quit."

"Wait. You were going to *quit*?"

He nodded. "I told you. We were only going to get one tuba."

He *had* told her. This whole time, she'd been

angry at him for so many things, but especially for not listening to her, and here she'd done the same thing to him.

Maybe they were both doing the best they could.

But she didn't have time to say anything else because the door swung open and five more people ran into the secret room. Frenchie was the first, still wearing the sousaphone, followed closely by the four members of Science Club.

"*Science Club?*" Louise said incredulously.

"Where's—" Frenchie started, but then her eyes rested on the sousaphone in the fierce embrace of the bear, and her eyes got huge. "—*WINSTON*?"

"I'm over here!" said Winston, waving his arms to get her attention. "I'm fine! I can go outside if I need to. I'd just...rather not walk *across* the room."

The bear, responding to the noise, rolled over and scooted back. Now the tuba was spooning the bear.

Everyone was quiet.

Everyone except the bear in the sound system.

Then Desirée spoke. "This doesn't seem like a statistically optimal situation."

All of Science Club was wearing Kittentown Dynamo shirts and sparkly cat ears, and none of it made them look any less serious.

"We were at the show," Tib explained.

"I see," said Louise.

"Bear-wise, I have the handouts from that wild animal unit we did in fourth grade," Desirée said, pulling out her computer. "I scan everything," she added modestly.

"I don't think we need to defend ourselves anymore," Louise said. "Something about either the tuba, the sandwich, or the recording has made the bear super chill. We need to focus on getting her to the protesters out front."

"Wait. What?" asked Winston.

"Once we get the bear to them, they get her to the wildlife sanctuary."

"And they know you're coming?"

"Not... exactly."

Winston looked worried. "Um..."

"It would have been easier if the bear was in the cage—" Her stomach sank. She knew what they were all thinking. The bear wasn't in the cage anymore.

"Or we could let this be somebody else's problem." Frenchie's eyes were still a little wild. "IT IS A BEAR. WE ARE IN MIDDLE SCHOOL."

"It just seems really chill right now," Louise said, trying to think of something. Anything.

"It was chasing Winston to kill him," Frenchie countered.

"It only looked like that," Winston jumped in. "She just wanted my bologna sandwich."

Frenchie looked at Winston, and her expression slowly softened. "Well, maybe."

The door opened, and everyone in the room froze as a voice said, "It's really safer for you in the Ursa Major Rotunda, ma'am, at least until we find the—" The security guard, who was now several steps into the room, broke off.

"The bear!" cried Kittentown Dynamo, delighted. She clapped her hands together.

The bodyguards, who had been following behind, all filed into the room and tried to form a protective barricade around her. "Stop, stop, stop, get out of my way," she said, pushing them aside.

Next to her, the security guard frantically fumbled with a spray bottle, finally got it up between him and the bear, and then sprayed himself in the face with it. He made a small, high-pitched noise and fell to his knees.

"What happened to him?" asked Frenchie, taking a step back.

"Homemade pepper spray," said Louise and the security guard at the same time.

"How did you...?" Frenchie couldn't seem to find the words.

Louise sniffed the air, confirming her suspicions. "I don't know where he learned about it, but we had a whole unit in fourth grade."

"Don't help me—help *him*," Kittentown Dynamo said, pushing her bodyguards over to help the security guard, who now had tears streaming down his face. The pop star barely seemed to notice—she only had eyes for the bear. "Look how sweet it is with that tuba," she said. "I knew the tubas would be a big hit."

Louise turned to say something about the pepper spray to the rest of Science Club and realized that every one of them was currently in silent stages of freaking out about Kittentown Dynamo. Everything had been happening so quickly, she forgot for a moment. Kittentown Dynamo was standing right there with them.

Wait.

She had an idea. "Ms. Dynamo?" Louise asked. "How would you feel about helping the bear get to freedom?"

"That sounds SO me," she gushed. "I mean, a bear is basically a very big cat and I am all about cats' rights."

"Er...," Tib began.

"Um...," said Eleni.

"Well...," started Desirée.

"That is not quite...," Vi said.

But then the prospect of correcting Kittentown Dynamo was too much for them and they all just nodded and made approving sounds.

"And you have a pretty big tour bus?"

"I have four!" Kittentown Dynamo said. "I like having options."

Louise crossed her mental fingers. "Do you think maybe we could use one of the buses to sneak this bear out of here and get her to a sanctuary for wildlife?"

"I'd be honored," she said, beaming at the bear.

"I believe I can help," came a voice from the floor. It was the security guard. He was lying down, and one of the bodyguards was fanning his face. "I think I'm okay now."

They all watched as he pulled himself back up to standing, swaying just a bit. The bodyguard steadied him.

"Sorry for that," he said, shaking his head

vigorously. "But if anybody needs a very good recipe for homemade pepper spray, I have one."

"You just have that spray bottle on you all the time?" asked Frenchie.

"Lately anyway," he said, shrugging. "The internet says pepper spray is very effective for keeping away bears."

"Only *until it dries*," Louise said, her hands on her hips. "Then they actually *like* the smell of it. You can't let it dry. Did no one else here go to fourth grade?"

Tib, Vi, and Desirée all raised a hand.

Eleni looked regretful. "I skipped that one."

The bear chose that moment to look up at the security guard, who froze.

"Don't let it dry," said Louise.

He sprayed himself in the face again, dropped to his knees, and made a noise that sounded like a very faraway scream.

"You were saying?" Winston prompted the guard after a moment. "You could help?"

The security guard attempted to smile and said, "I—HOOO, sorry—wasn't ready yet." He took a shaky breath. "I'll scrub the security cameras so there's no record of you getting the bear out."

"Why?" Louise asked suspiciously.

The man shrugged. "Let's say I'm doing it for the bear."

Louise wasn't sure they could trust him, but then again he had sprayed himself with pepper spray when she told him to, so maybe he was a reasonable guy.

The guard pulled himself back up and said, "The bear will just have disappeared as far as they know."

Louise caught Winston's eye for just a second. A good disappearance. That was what they needed.

"Thanks," Winston said.

"But how do we get the bear on the bus?" Frenchie asked.

There was a long silence, and they all watched as the bear licked the sousaphone a couple times and resumed snuggling it.

Louise heard a rustling and turned to see Eleni root through her bag, pull out a bag of cookies.

"I brought these?" Eleni said, offering Louise the tinfoil package. "I know this isn't the right moment, but we tried the bake sale stuff again Friday, when you didn't come to Science Club. Dr. O said you were taking a break? But we can talk about that later, I guess. Anyway, we used the right oven this time and made a lot of really good cookies. These are peanut butter. It looks like maybe we don't need to buy tubas anymore"—she gestured toward the sousaphones—"so I think we'll have a lot of money for supplies! But, so, maybe they could be useful for motivating the bear?"

Louise took the package and smelled them. She broke a cookie in half and threw it near the bear.

Nothing happened at first. But then the bear's nose started twitching. Its eyes opened. Everyone took a step back as the bear inched toward the half cookie. The bear nudged it and then ate the whole thing in one giant lick.

"Okay," said Louise. "I think we've got a way to motivate the bear."

"We're just going to leave a trail of cookies all the way to the tour bus?" Frenchie asked. "There's no way we aren't going to get caught."

"And I don't think I brought enough cookies," Eleni said, a worried look on her face. "Sorry. I wasn't thinking ahead."

"You did great, Eleni," Louise said. "We just need something closer than the tour bus."

Everyone was quiet for a second.

"What if—" Winston's face lit up. "What if we disguise it?"

"As a sousaphone player?" Frenchie asked. "That might be tricky."

Winston looked at Kittentown Dynamo. "How much room is there in your giant cat head?"

Thankfully, the pop star had no problem turning her huge prop into a temporary bear den, and while the bodyguards brought the cat head from the field where they'd left it, Louise sent Winston and Frenchie to speak with the teachers. They were going to be needed for one last performance.

Once everyone was in place, and the cat head sat just outside the room, Louise laid a careful trail of peanut butter cookies up and into it. Everyone held their breaths, but then the bear pleasantly obliged, lumbering from one cookie to the next, climbing up into the mouth and down, where Louise had dumped the rest of the cookies.

As soon as the bear was at the bottom of the cat head, Kittentown Dynamo gently closed the lid.

"Now you guys carry it out," Louise instructed the pop star's bodyguards.

They looked unsure. "How do we know it won't

come out and eat us while we're carrying it?" one of them asked.

"Fair," Winston said.

"I guess we don't," Louise said.

At that, the security guard said, "Ooh!" He jumped forward, spraying the pepper spray around the outside. "That way, she won't *want* to come out until she gets there, when it's dry."

They stepped into place, but before they could heft it up in the air, tears began streaming down their cheeks. The bodyguards were all . . . crying.

"Hey, hey, hey," Kittentown Dynamo said comfortingly. "You don't *have* to do this."

The closest one shook his head. "It's the pepper spray. It's *really* strong."

"But thank you," said another. "It's nice to have choices."

Then, muscles bulging, the bodyguards struggled to lift the cat. "The bear . . . is . . . heavier than we're used to," one of them grunted.

"I know you can do it!" encouraged Kittentown Dynamo.

They did, although tears ran down their faces as they shuffled along the halls of the stadium and out through the front entrance, where the teachers, still dressed as kittens, were making a tunnel all the way to the four tour buses. The teachers danced enthusiastically, distracting the Kittentown Dynamo fans from noticing that the bodyguards were having a difficult time. Everyone was doing a really terrible, wonderful job.

Louise wanted to watch the procession, but she had something else to take care of. She ran around to the other end of the stadium entrance, where a small crowd gathered.

"Louise!" called a familiar voice. "Over here!"

She found Carlyle at the center of the group, blowing gently onto a new coffee. He smiled at her. "I saw you earlier and hoped you'd come back! Want to carry a sign? Mina had to leave early, and so—"

She shook her head, interrupting. "Where's Gwen?"

He tipped his head toward the coffee truck, back again, and Louise dragged him over. Gwen was just getting her own new coffee but peered at Louise over the rim of the paper cup. "Louise! Would you like some—"

"You've got the brochures? Great. I need you to come with me. You can bring the coffee." Louise began walking quickly back toward the tour buses, and then, when she realized she was alone, looked back. They were following slowly, hunched over the steaming drinks and stepping carefully to avoid spilling. "Okay, new plan," she said, jogging back to them, grabbing the coffees and throwing them in a nearby trash can. "You can't bring the coffee."

"Louise!" Gwen gasped.

They looked at the trash can sadly, but Louise stepped behind them, pushing them in the right direction. "Just look normal," she said.

"Louise, what is going on?" Carlyle sounded worried.

"Everything is fine," Louise reassured them. "I've stolen the bear and I need you to escort it to the wildlife refuge from the brochures, because if I don't eventually go home tonight, my mom is going to be suspicious. Well, maybe. Maybe not, to be honest. But I think this will all go a lot more smoothly if you chaperone the situation."

"I'm sorry, *what situation*?" Gwen asked at the same time that Carlyle said, "You stole the bear?"

"Yeah, yeah, maybe don't say it so loud." They were almost at the tour bus. Fans milled around, hoping to get a glimpse of Kittentown Dynamo, and beyond them, a solid line of teachers danced and meowed, making it hard to clearly see the giant cat head as it moved forward in fits and starts. The bodyguards were just a couple of yards away from the bus. *"You can do it,"* she said under her breath.

"Excuse us," she said out loud, pushing Carlyle and Gwen through the fans, and then between two computer science teachers. "Guests of Kittentown Dynamo coming through."

"Guests of *who*?" asked Carlyle, trying to turn around to look at Louise.

But they'd reached the front of the tour bus, and Louise tapped on the door just as the bodyguards made their way around back, where the cat head—plus bear—could be loaded into the compartment usually reserved for the gear.

The front door slid open, they climbed on, and the bus driver, who had a slightly terrified expression on his face, shut it behind them, muting the noise from outside.

The bus driver tried to smile at Louise, but it didn't work—he definitely looked like a man who had just been told that he was about to be the getaway driver for a bear-stealing operation.

The tour bus was huge, like a house on wheels,

and Louise led the way into a living room area. Kittentown Dynamo, now in jeans and a T-shirt, bounced up from a polka-dotted sofa.

"Carlyle, Gwen, this is Kittentown Dynamo."

"Kitty, please," Kittentown said, shaking hands with the two of them. Their mouths were hanging open. "Have a seat!"

They all sat down, except for Louise, who turned to the two protesters and asked in one breath, "Are you okay making a trip to the wildlife refuge right now to deliver the bear, who is about to be loaded onto this bus?"

They looked at each other. Carlyle still seemed too shocked to speak. Gwen turned back to Louise with a huge smile. "You bet we are."

"Great. Kitty, you can fill them in on everything?"

Kittentown Dynamo nodded.

And with that, Louise ran back off the bus, giving the bus driver one last encouraging look from the ground before he shut the door.

She had done it.

The fans, having given up on Kittentown Dynamo sightings, were drifting off into the night, and teachers were starting to head back into the stadium, probably to change out of their kitten outfits. She let herself be carried along with them, until she got to the entranceway.

The security guard stood by the door, his phone to his ear. He held up a finger, asking her to wait.

Louise stopped and stood next to him.

"No, sir," he was saying. "We don't have a status update on the bear.... Yes, sir, I understand that it is humiliating for the team to lose the mascot in the stadium during a game." He listened for a minute and then looked up at the tour bus in front of them, engine running. "I believe Kittentown Dynamo has already left the premises. I'll see what I can find out, sir." He ended the call.

The two of them stood in silence for a moment, until the bus finally turned on its headlights and pulled out. Kittentown Dynamo's other three buses followed.

"Good job, little Volpe," the man finally said.

She gaped at him.

"Yeah, I know who you are." He looked down at her and cleared his throat. "I know *all* about who you are."

"Oh," she said.

They went back to looking out after the bus, like

maybe they'd see it still driving away. After a minute, he said, "Did you know I knew your father?"

Louise's breath caught.

"I thought maybe you didn't," he said, leaning back against the building. "He was my friend."

She didn't know what to say.

"We spent a lot of time together, mostly waiting for the right time to run out to his car, that sort of thing. But I'd say my favorite story about him happened even before I'd met him. Want to hear it?"

Louise nodded.

"I'd just been promoted to the night shift. Before that, I was part-time, so this was a big deal. And I was nervous about it because I wasn't used to staying up all night. I didn't want to do anything embarrassing like fall asleep. But I walked into the office my first night, and I guess the other guard on nights back then—her name was Anelle—she could tell what was going on, because she said, 'You don't have a thing to worry about. We have a fairy godmother.'

"Then she shows me, in a corner of the office I'd never noticed before. There was a *really* fancy coffee machine, and a whole cupboard stocked with different kinds of coffees and espressos. Anelle says, 'Somebody's been sending the security office all this coffee. We used to have to drink that stuff'—she pointed to some instant mix—'but now we've got the real deal. You won't have any problem staying awake.' And she was right. I loved night shift. It was peaceful, and every night I looked forward to the most delicious coffee.

"Later I was promoted again, to daytimes, and the coffee kept coming. I always wondered who sent it. For a while, I thought it was my boss. But the bosses came and went. And it definitely wasn't the owner. That man wouldn't spend a nickel he didn't have to spend, not on an employee."

"How'd you find out it was my dad?" Louise asked.

"You already know how this ends, huh?"

"I deduced it."

"You're right, of course. But I learned by accident. He never meant for me to find out." A look Louise knew crossed his face. "Later, you know, before he disappeared? He wasn't remembering so well."

"Yeah," she said quietly.

"Well, I guess he remembered that he needed to order that coffee, but he didn't remember how to do it. He called my number and tried to place an order." His voice was getting gruff. "I let him."

"That was nice of you," Louise said softly.

He paused for a minute, and Louise leaned into him a bit. "And then I called and placed the order myself. He'd have appreciated that, I think."

Louise waited until her voice was steady. "I think so, too."

He wiped his nose on his sleeve, and then his phone rang. He looked at the screen and turned it off. The crowd had completely cleared by now, and the lights buzzed overhead. "So you're a detective or a scientist?"

She looked at him.

"Making deductions?"

"Oh," she said. "Scientist. Winston seems to be the detective of the family."

"Science is cool."

"I know."

"Your dad would be proud."

She smiled and looked up, where the stars would be if the stadium lights weren't so bright. Weren't their own complete, imperfect galaxy.

"I know."

CHAPTER 28

WINSTON SAT ON the front stoop.

He was wearing his sousaphone, hoping it didn't rumple the jacket he was wearing. He'd decided not to go full suit ("It's *Aquarium Night*," Louise had said. "It's not even prom. You need some chill."), and so he was wearing a purple shirt, a dark blue jacket, his nice jeans, and turquoise sneakers. He wore a tie, too, one that his mom had made special for him. It was a plaid tie, something she'd thrifted, but she'd sewn a tuba on at the bottom, with big, bright stitches that stood out against the rest of his outfit. He hoped Frenchie approved. The sun had already set, and it was chilly out—if he was smart, he'd be wearing his coat, but he wanted her to get the full effect.

Next to him was a small baggie of chopped-up pineapple.

She'd be over to get him soon. Then they'd walk to school together, and the buses would take them over to the aquarium.

It had taken him approximately two minutes to get ready, probably because he was so nervous, so with all this extra time, he'd taken the sousaphone outside to wait. He played "The Imperial March" quietly.

He'd only been sitting there for a few minutes, when Louise ran up and stood in front of him proudly.

"Guess who's going to the statewide science competition?" she said, a giant smile on her face.

"You are?"

"I AM," she said.

"I'm shocked," he said.

"Kitty gave me an idea for a project, and it got accepted!" Since that day at the stadium, Louise had been on a first-name basis with Kittentown Dynamo. "She was giving me the latest update on the bear, and how she's adapting to life at the sanctuary—she spends most of her time rolling around in the leaves, by the way—and then Kitty started telling me about sound waves, and now I'm going to present on the science of sound waves in water, and how different sounds make different, perfectly geometric fractals in the water, like snowflakes."

"Wow," said Winston. "That's pretty cool."

"I know," said Louise, sinking onto the step next to Winston.

The wind rustled the tree out front, and a few red and yellow leaves floated to the ground. "What about..." Winston hesitated, not sure if it was okay to talk about. "The cure? What you did out there on the field?"

Louise leaned over her knees to play with a shoelace. "I don't know," she said. "Dr. O ran a few tests, but she still can't tell why it happened. She thinks it might be like how adrenaline makes people able to lift a car if it's on their loved one or something. That when the bear went for you—or really the bologna—that my adrenaline amped up my normal metabolic bioluminescence."

"You went superhuman because you have such strong feelings for bologna?" Winston said.

"Yeah," Louise said. "That's probably what happened."

"Probably," Winston agreed. He noodled through "The Imperial March" again, quietly, and then fell silent as the wind rustled down the street. He was sure he smelled chocolate in the air. The past and future were all tangled up, and maybe they'd never get separated. But maybe that was how it was supposed to be. "I had a thought, Lou."

"Yeah?"

He took a shaky breath. "I think we need to have a funeral. For Dad."

She didn't say anything.

"But really, like, for us. I think I need to say goodbye to him somehow. Would you be okay with that?"

Louise was quiet for another minute. Then she said, "You know something interesting?"

"Huh," said Winston.

"Shrimps," she said, swinging her backpack off and in front of her. She reached in and dug through. "There's these shrimp. Snapping shrimp. They're called snapping shrimp because they have this one extra-big claw that they use to make snapping noises. Except that's just how *our* ears hear the noise. It's not snapping to the shrimp. To the shrimp, it's this intense pressure wave. It's how they fight. They face off, and they snap those claws and send underwater pressure waves at their enemies. It's, like, the shrimp version of a sonic boom."

"Why do you know this?"

"I read about it," she said, pulling out the package of bologna.

"Uh-huh."

"That sonic boom should rock the shrimp's brain. The shrimp should be getting concussions nonstop, just by going about their average, snappy day."

"But they don't?" Winston asked.

"They don't," Louise said. She took a piece of bologna and put it on her head. "They've developed a protein shield over their head. It absorbs the shock. It keeps things quiet inside."

Winston took a piece of the bologna and put it on his head. It was cool against his forehead and weirdly calming.

They sat like that for a moment, and then Louise said, "We can do a funeral."

"Okay."

"Okay."

"I'm probably going to need to play 'The Imperial March,'" Winston warned her.

"I think Dad would understand," Louise said. "And anyway, I'm probably going to have a lot to say."

"I can't wait," Winston said, giving her a sousaphone-sized nudge.

She leaned over her knees and traced an invisible line on the step, connecting the leaves that had scattered there. "Win?"

"Yeah?"

"Where do you think he is?"

Winston took a breath and blew it through the sousaphone, but so lightly that it didn't make any music. It just sounded like the wind, or maybe the inside of a shell. "Do you mean, where do I really think he is, or where do I imagine he is?"

She hesitated. "Where do you imagine he is?"

Winston nodded. "I looked up the real center of the galaxy."

She made a small noise, and he knew that she understood why.

"Turns out it's a super-massive black hole approximately twenty-eight kilolight-years away in outer space. When I need to know where he is, I picture him traveling twenty-eight kilolight-years away to visit the other center of the galaxy so that he can bring it hot dogs and make it a little better. What about you?"

"I imagine that he's out on the lake," she said. "It's right after sunset, and he's floating on the water. And his molecules are part of the lake and the lake's molecules are part of the sky, and they're all the same thing."

"I like that," Winston said.

"I like the hot dog thing," Louise replied.

"What hot dog thing?" asked Frenchie, who had appeared on the sidewalk in front of the house.

And Winston promptly forgot how to talk.

She was gorgeous.

She was wearing a midnight-blue dress, sleeveless, that came right to her knees. She always wore pants—Winston realized he'd never seen her knees before, and his face went hot.

"I got you flowers," he said awkwardly, handing over the baggie. "*A* flower. I got you a few pieces of flower." This was a disaster. He should have practiced this.

She burst out laughing.

"Technically, a pineapple is part of a flowering plant, but not the flower itself," Louise whispered.

Winston shot her what he considered a very deadly look and then turned back to Frenchie. "I thought we could eat them on the way over," he said.

"It's great," she said, and then handed the bag back. "I just need to do one thing before we go. Louise?"

And to Winston's surprise, Louise hopped up, the two of them climbed the stairs together, and they disappeared into the house. He couldn't imagine what Frenchie needed Lou for, but he didn't mind waiting a few more minutes. He'd been nervous asking Louise about the funeral, but it'd gone fine. Maybe they'd make it a big party, he thought. Dad would have loved that.

And then there was a noise behind him, and he stood and turned to see Frenchie in the doorway. She'd put Louise's glow stuff on the parts of her skin that had lost their pigment and gone white, and now she looked like an actual living constellation.

He realized all at once that she was the center of his galaxy.

And he had no idea how he'd been so lucky to end up here, out of the whole Milky Way.

"I'll just take this," said Louise, helping him take off the sousaphone.

"Careful...," Winston said, still unable to take his eyes off Frenchie.

"Obviously I'll be careful." It sounded like Louise was rolling her eyes.

“You ready to go?” Frenchie asked.

“I’m ready.” Winston’s voice cracked. He didn’t even care. “You ready to look at some sharks?”

“I am *so* ready,” she said as they started to walk down the sidewalk. “But...is that sandwich meat on your head? You trying to be bait?”

Winston tore the bologna off, shooting Louise a backward glance. No bologna. She must’ve taken hers off before Frenchie noticed. Of course. Louise smirked as he ran back and handed her the slice.

“Say hi to the jellyfish for me,” she said to him.

“Just for that, I’m not telling the jellyfish anything.”

“They don’t have ears anyway,” she said, smiling.

“You’re the worst.”

“Love you, too.”

And with that, the two sousaphone players of Subito began the walk to school.

CHAPTER 29

FIVE MINUTES AFTER they'd left, Louise watched as her mom's car screeched to a stop in front of the house. She got out, her hair wild, her bag spilling pens out along the sidewalk as she ran toward the front door. She stopped when she saw Louise on the stoop.

"I missed them?" she asked.

"You missed them," Louise confirmed.

Her mom deflated a little and then joined Louise on the stoop.

"Mom," Louise said, "Do you know the scientific method?"

"It's been a while, but I think I remember it," she said, pulling her hair back into a knot.

"First you ask yourself a question," Louise said. "Like, for example, am I good at being a real estate agent?"

There was a very long pause.

"I'm not sure I like where this is going."

"Well," Louise said as she squared her shoulders, the ones that were made to stop things, just like her father's had been, "scientists have to ask the hard questions. Do you even *like* being a real estate agent? Do you like having to work all those extra hours?"

"Oh," her mom said softly.

"What?"

"Louise—" She stopped and rubbed her forehead. "I'm not doing real estate stuff in the evenings."

Louise started. "Then what are you—"

"I've been going to grieving groups. For people who lost their spouses." She looked away.

Louise just waited.

"You and Winston are doing so well. And I... I'm not. It's like Dad's everywhere. I can't sell any houses, because when I see a happy couple, I start crying, and nobody wants to buy a house from somebody who can't walk them through the front door without bursting into tears."

This was not what Louise had expected at all. Dr. O had been right. Sometimes there are factors that you don't take into consideration.

"I just felt like if I could get better on my own, you wouldn't have to worry about me. You spent enough of your life already worrying about Dad."

Louise thought for a second. "Mom, do you know anything about magnets?"

Her mom looked sideways at her. "Is this going to be another dig at how bad I am at selling houses?" she said with a crooked smile.

Louise shook her head. "When a magnet gets weak, it's not like it's permanently broken. You can fix it. You just have to put it next to a stronger magnet, and then it gets stronger, too."

Her mom took a raggedy breath. "You are very wise, kiddo."

"Winston and I are doing okay, I think, now. But we need you here." She let her mom think about that for a second and then she added, "Also, we are literally *turning into* bologna. I mean, we need you for other reasons, too, but definitely that part."

Her mom was crying a little bit now, and Louise scooted closer to her. "Mom, we're gonna be okay. Also?"

"Yeah?"

"Cocoa punch," she said, giving her a solid whammy to the shoulder.

"Ow!" And her mom, who had barely even smiled for two whole years, burst out laughing, tears still on her face. She wrapped one arm around her daughter, who burrowed close.

Louise could have stayed like that all night. She took a deep breath of the sweet, chocolatey air. It was funny—she couldn't remember ever smelling it here. She always thought they lived too far for the smell to travel. Maybe they did, and this was something special, a ghost wind, to help them remember how to be okay again.

Maybe, Louise thought as she leaned against her mom, *maybe that's all ghosts are. Remembering.* She thought of her dad, playing like he was Pac-Man, chased around their house by ghosts.

She didn't think she believed in ghosts, scientifically, at least. But maybe they weren't *supposed* to be scientific. Maybe they were just the memories of a person you knew, like your dad, who would never have left if he could have helped it.

Or the memory of a home that you once had, like the forest, that stays in you, even when you get stuck in a cage for so many years you can't remember what leaves feel like or other bears sound like.

Or the memory of a few notes, played on a tuba, that make you know that a person you love is just around the corner.

So close.

Always, always so close.

ACKNOWLEDGMENTS

For a book about teams—about how hard it is to be on them, and also how they can save our lives—this story has been lucky enough to be part of a lot of spectacular teams.

Thanks to the VCFA community, who first heard a chapter about a kid and a bear ten years ago and asked me all the best questions.

Thanks to everybody who helped me better understand CTE and brains and chemistry, especially Dr. Annabelle Singer, Dr. Dan Speiser, and Dr. Arvela Heider. Thanks to Leah Roberson, my tuba and sousaphone expert.

Thanks to the brilliant editorial team that took the story into the end zone: Rotem Moscovich, Heather Crowley, Abby Ranger, Ruqayyah Daud, and Liz Kossnar, as well as Jacqueline Hornberger, whose copyediting notes included pointing out a joke I hadn't even realized I'd made, which I'm pretty sure makes it officially her joke now.

I'm deeply indebted to everybody who read (or listened to) early drafts, including Eden Robins, Sadieh Rifai, Rachel Wilson, Laurie Morrison Fabius, Cordelia Jensen, Laura Sibson, Larissa Theule, Steve Bramucci, the Beverly Shores folks, and the Gardeners. If I've been to your house in the last ten years, I've probably secretly worked on it there, so this one really goes out to everybody. Thanks, pals!

Thanks to Rachel Hylton, who reads with more brains and heart than anybody I've ever known and who still quotes a line I cut from the very first draft.

Thanks to Tina Dubois, agent of my dreams.

Thanks to my folks for the original team.

Thanks to Jorin for the new one.